Laugh Anyway Mom

Hilarious survival stories from a MOTHER OF FIVE
who has learned how to keep the joy in
motherhood and how you can too!

Tracy DeGraaf

Look who's talking about *Laugh Anyway Mom!*

"I have to tell you that **this book is fantastic**!!! I found myself reading stories while waiting in the car when my son was at soccer practice or at the office when I just wanted a good laugh. Thanks for writing about these experiences as they will help **encourage mothers everywhere** regardless of how many children she's blessed with."
— Veronica Romero Executive Assistant to Jack Canfield

"Tracy DeGraaf beautifully captures the hysterical highs and lows of motherhood through her colorful yet transparent tales. **A must read for any mom**."
— Amy Pedersen, Author of *The Miracle of Me*

"*Laugh Anyway Mom* is **HILARIOUS**! Tracy has a way of turning a phrase that tickles the senses and loosens that giggle bone."
— Ginger Brashinger, Columnist and mother of an over active son.

"Don't miss this chance to get a **LAUGHTER-FILLED** glimpse of growing up with boys-boys-boys! I have a new appreciation for my mother's perspective on all of us surviving childhood!"
— David W. Ping, author of *OUTFLOW: Outward Focused Living in a Self-focused World*.

"*Laugh Anyway Mom* is A **MUST READ FOR ALL MOMS** past, present, and future!"
— Debby Doig, Author, Life & Executive Coach, Leadership Developer.

"*This book* will make you **laugh at the priceless stories of raising kids**."
—Valerie Monahan, Kindergarten Teacher & Mother of 3.

"Every woman will be able to relate to Tracy DeGraaf's LAUGH-OUT-LOUD real life adventures we call Motherhood! **EXTREMELY ENTERTAINING!**"
— Diana Pratt, mother of 3 grown men and grandmother of 2.

"*Laugh Anyway Mom* is both **funny and right on the mark**. You must read this book!"
— Scott Stratton D.C. Chiropractor and dad to 5 sons.

"To imagine raising five boys can be **frightening**; to read about it in *Laugh Anyway Mom* is **hilarious**."
— Walter Pickup, Contributing Writer to Christianity Today International

"Tracy DeGraaf tells her story **entertaining** the reader with precarious-turned-hilarious situations!"
— Cathrine Schipman, mother of 3 and next door neighbor to the DeGraaf's.

"I am a 43-year-old woman who has never had children. After reading this book, I now know why! Tracy shows how she **raised her children with laughter and humor** as well."
— Angela Riccio, Actress/Comedian

"If you are craving **simpler times** and a good **belly laugh**, this is a must-read!"
— Lara Vander Ploeg, Author/Radio Personality

"It's **comforting** to know that I'm not alone and that other moms are facing the same challenges. All moms **will appreciate this cleverly written tale!**"
— Sue Davis, busy mom of two boys

"What a **bundle of laughs**! In her Martha-Stewart-free house, the joys of raising a big family become real."
— Rebecca Palumbo, Mom of 2 and Principal/Creative Director of Rollins Palumbo Creative.

"*Laugh Anyway Mom* is not only **refreshing and comical**, but also tells a story of what moms are made of, and **how to keep your sense of humor** while juggling all the mishaps that come with the job!"
— Dana Saller, mom of 3 grown boys.

"*Laugh Anyway Mom* is a **delightfully funny and honest look at life** in a big family. Tracy shares the meaning of life that is experienced through the daily fears, frustrations, and joys of motherhood."
— Nancy Sink, Pre-School Director and Mother of 3 and Grandmother of 6.

"*Laugh Anyway Mom* reminds us that **parenting is meant to be an adventure**, not an exercise, and it's a lot more fun when we don't take ourselves too seriously."
— Gina Beltrami, Mom of 4 and co-creator of the song, *I Farted on Santa's Lap (Now Christmas is Gonna Stink for Me)*

"From emergency rooms to bathrooms to making room in your heart for your kids, Tracy's **hilarious** tales and related take home advice will have **you laughing, crying, learning, and loving.**"
— Karen Ehman, national speaker for Proverbs 31 Ministries and Hearts at Home Conferences; author of several books including *The Complete Guide to Getting and Staying Organized*; wife and home schooling mom of 3.

Dedication

In loving memory of my mom, Joan Rose Lopez Moran
August 9, 1941 – May 29, 1993

"Time waits for no one!"

This was taken on my graduation day from Illinois State University in 1988. My mom is the one with her tongue out. I am the one laughing!

Contents

Acknowledgments

Thank you to my husband and my best friend, Ron, for making me laugh and letting me cry.

Thanks to my children Nathan, Luke, Joel, Adam, and Caleb, who give me a lot to write about! You guys literally ROCK! You bring me true JOY, and my crowning achievement in life will always be my family. (It's really okay that sometimes it's a thorny crown. That's what makes life worth laughing about!) Thank you to all of my family who have supported me along the way!

Thank you to those who have given direction in so many ways, my dad, "Butch" Moran, who always sees the glass half full! Debby Doig, Jim Thompson, Tracey Trottenberg, Maria Simone, Diana Flegal, Steve Harrison, Bill Harrison, Teri Hawkins, Michael Issac, Donna Dahl, Dr. Scott Stratton, Jennifer Rundall, Diana Pratt, Jeni Ozark, and Janet and Landy DeField.

Thanks to George Foster, Kellie Mize, and Kim Carter. Your graphic design talents made this project so much better! Thanks for being so gracious and patient with the many revisions! I highly recommend your services to anyone who wants to work with extremely talented AND genuinely gracious people!

Thank you to Susan Epperson and Elizabeth Ridley, my editors whose honest feedback made all the difference.

Thanks also to Cindy Hart for proofing!

Thank you to Lara Vander Ploeg and Scott Buhrmaster for your wisdom and direction and for leading me to Bill and Steve Harrison's Quantum Leap Program for authors, speakers and entrepreneurs. That program is the BEST!

Thank you to all who spent time reading and evaluating this project and wrote such kind testimonials of support!

Thanks to all of my friends who read and re-read chapters. And, a very big prayer of gratitude to God for the blessings in my life which are too numerous to count!!!

Foreword

By Debby Doig

Here are some of the thoughts that come to mind when I think of raising five boys. Having my tubes tied at the onset of puberty. Becoming a nun. Prozac. Looking like I was dressed up for Halloween on a daily basis. And the value of cloistered monasteries that accept boys at preschool age and keep them until their twenty-first birthday. By that age you would hope they were at least potty trained.

My perspective shifted after meeting Tracy DeGraaf. I must confess that I thought I misheard her when she said she was the mom of five boys. Her lipstick was on her lips, her mascara on her eyelashes. Her hair was brushed and in place and all the buttons of her blouse were in the right buttonholes. As hard as I tried, I could not see any visible signs of shell shock. So I listened closer convinced that her words would reveal the tumultuous impact of sharing a home with five boys and a husband. Instead, what I heard were the experiences of a woman whose life tickled her own funny bone.

Spirit, spirited, and spiritual are the threads that Tracy weaves through the stories in *LAUGH ANYWAY MOM*. Although the stories she shares are uproariously funny and refreshingly real, it is more than just a funny book with funny stories about being a mom. This book is about the experience of being human. Through the telling of her tales with unique wit, Tracy shows us what it means to be awake to life even on the days she is dealing with eggshells in the sink, dirty underwear scowls, or a Mrs. Kravitz, the kind of neighbor we have all had. The stories are about a mom, a wife, a woman, and her family. They show us that each of us has what it takes to meet all the experiences in our lives, even when they are filled with *UGH!*™ moments.

LAUGH ANYWAY MOM is an invitation that opens the door to Tracy's home. With her heart and her humor, she invites us in to see her dirty laundry, daily dilemmas, her challenges, and her triumphs. Most of all the book and its author invite us to experience what the stories teach best...the extraordinary joy in ordinary moments.

Introduction
(Don't skip this—it's hilarious!)

How to Guarantee a Vasectomy!

"Call the doctor for me today, okay, babe?" my husband, Ron, said as he bent over to lace up his work boots. He had a nagging pain in his foot (a neuroma), and he knew it was time to get a shot of cortisone to calm things down. As a heavy equipment operator, he was on his feet a lot getting on and off of tractors. He worked hard and needed his feet to be in good shape to keep doing so.

I loaded the last sippy-cup into the dishwasher, poured in some detergent, and shut the door. I turned to Ron as the dishwasher started to hum—music to my ears. I was wearing an old nightshirt that barely fit around my eight-months pregnant middle. I was thirty-five-years old, and we were expecting our fifth baby. We had been blessed with four sons and I was sure that THIS ONE HAD TO BE A GIRL. After all, what were the odds of having five boys? We didn't necessarily plan any of the pregnancies, but we were bad at prevention—*really bad!*

"Okay," I said and kissed him good-bye. He left for work and left me at home with my very pregnant belly and four sleeping sons. Sleep was a double-edged sword for my boys. I loved it when they were all down for the count, but knew they were only refueling. But for the moment, the early morning quiet was enjoyable. I sat down with a giant cup of coffee. My doctor told me to cut back on caffeine because of the pregnancy. I went out and bought the biggest coffee cup I could find. I poured in half a pot and called it my "one cup in the morning."

This pregnancy was grueling. It seemed each day brought a new pain in the apple-cheeks. I knew this would be my last child. It wasn't a decision that I had to think about, pray over, or even make a list of the pros and cons. I never even broached the subject with Ron, because I knew that I was DONE.

As the day progressed, my boys were in usual form—rambunctious. My oldest, Nate, was eleven and in fourth grade. Son #2, Luke, was ten and in third. Son #3, Joel, was four and in preschool. And, son #4, Adam, was two and in EVERYTHING! They were all home that day. It was mid-February and schools in Illinois were closed in observance of Presidents' Day. (When I was a kid, we got the same day off, but we called it "Lincoln's Birthday." Only a dead president could get away with canceling school on a weekday in the Midwest in the middle of winter.) It was bitter cold outside, so when the boys got up, they were confined to the house. It was like being in a cage full of monkeys.

I was making progress on laundry, picking up the endless trail of stuff all over the house when I stopped mid-stride and smelled a wafting of "nasty" coming from my two-year-old's backside. Time for a change! I corralled my busy-as-a-bee boy, and flopped him to the floor for a quick cleanup.

"Adam stinks," he said in a moment of self-awareness.

"Yes," I replied, "and we need to start using the potty before the new baby comes, don't we, Adam?" I said.

A commercial for Viagra came on TV and the announcer said, "Ask your doctor about how you can…blah blah blah."

It reminded me to call the toe doctor for Ron. I finished up, fastened the tabs on Adam's disposable diaper, and slowly got my old pregnant self up off the floor.

"Do you need some help, Mom?" Nate asked.

"No," I grunted, "but thanks for the offer. I just need to take it slow and I can manage to get all of my parts upright."

Waddling through the kitchen to the garage, I disposed of the soiled diaper, washed my hands, then grabbed the phone book and opened it to "p" for physicians. As I searched the list of podiatrists, I could hear a fight breaking out in one of the boys' bedrooms.

"Give it back!"

"No, it's mine."

"It is not."

"BOYS! Knock it off, I'm on the phone!!" I screamed with the phone in the crook of my neck while still fumbling through the yellow pages. A crash followed my unheeded plea topped off with a cry of "I'M TELLING!"

Right there, in that chaotic moment, with the most clarity that I have ever had about family planning, I decided to forget about the "toe" doctor and move a bit north on the male anatomy. I flipped past the podiatrist pages and went straight to urology and made an appointment for my husband to get a vasectomy.

"Okay, Mrs. DeGraaf, we will see Ron on Friday at ten," said a voice that sounded like it belonged to an angel.

"Sounds good to me," I said, "but what if my husband won't go along with it?"

"Well," the voice chuckled, "he'll have to agree to have the surgical procedure, and sign some paperwork, or we can't do it," she said.

"I don't think we'll have a problem. See you on Friday," I said while "shhhh"-ing Joel who was at my side, tattling on Luke AGAIN. I hung up.

"WHAT is going on?" I asked my son.

"Luke took my Qui-Gon Jin," Joel said.

"Put the Star Wars stuff away, I have my own mission right now."

I had to convince my husband that a vasectomy was no big deal. I finished cleaning up the house but went the extra mile and used Pine-Sol to clean the floors. I told Nate to get the vacuum and give the living room a once-over.

"Luke," I called, interrupting his Star Wars battle, "get over here and put all these shoes away." We always had a pile of shoes at our door.

I wanted the house to be clean, the children well-behaved, and the food to be delicious. I got out my favorite cookbook and made a grocery list. I know how to get what I want from my husband—put something good in his stomach and he's putty in my hands. I loaded all the kids into the van and we went to the store. I made two main dishes, sides, and a dessert, a Herculean feat since my normal "going all out" was a frozen pizza with a self-rising crust. Who can cook with five boys underfoot? Not me!

But this was important, so I let the boys watch violent cartoons and eat dry sugar cereal in my bed just to keep them out of my way. I was serious, and needed to be left alone in the kitchen to work some magic!

When Ron came home, I was ready. I had showered, brushed my teeth, put on makeup, and did my hair. Dressed in a decent pair of jeans and a nice maternity top with no stains on the belly, I greeted the father of my children with a warm smile and a peck on the cheek.

"Wow," he said. "It smells good in here." The place *was* spotless and the meat was almost finished cooking. The house smelled like a nice combination of Pine-Sol and beef. A fresh pot of coffee was brewing and a fire had been lit in the fireplace. He should have known something was up.

I put the food on the table and called the kids. The six of us sat down for a really nice family dinner. Ron was the last to pull up his chair. He still had his long underwear on from work that day.

"This is great," he said, clueless about what was coming. He said a blessing over the food and we dug in.

"Trace, did you call the doctor today?" Ron asked.

"Yep," I said through a mouthful of mashed potatoes, not making eye contact.

"What did they say?"

"They can get you in on Friday," I said.

"What time?"

"You have to be there at ten. I'll drive you."

"Why do you have to drive me? It's just a shot of cortisone and I can drive myself and then go to work."

That was when I explained what *kind* of doctor he would be seeing on Friday and for what procedure. Finally, he caught on to my "June Cleaver" type perfect house and dinner.

"So, do you want to do it?" I asked.

"Do I WANT to? No, I can't say that I want to," he said.

"Okay, let me rephrase that," I said. "Do you want to do IT? And by do IT, I MEAN *IT*, because if you don't get a vasectomy, we won't be doing *IT* again!"

Ron agreed without much discussion, and we kept our Friday appointment. While he was getting the "procedure," I waited for him in the row of office chairs just outside the room. I tried to cross my legs, but couldn't because my giant thirty-seven-weeks-along belly was occupying my lap. I couldn't get comfortable. I had a strange and slightly vengeful feeling inside as I craned my head toward the room Ron was in and tried to hear what was going on in there. I heard voices and a little laughter and then he came out with a prescription in his hand. The doctor followed behind.

"That's it," the doctor said. "Take it easy over the weekend. Keep it iced and don't overdo it," he added as he slapped Ron on the back.

"Make sure that you bring in a sample in six weeks so we can double-check that everything went okay," the nurse instructed.

That was it? I couldn't believe it. No screaming? No counting backward from ten? No concentrating on an object on the wall and breathing slowly? What a rip-off. I wanted to at least see a bead of sweat on my husband's brow. I expected him to come out of there looking like he had just dismounted his horse after a six-month journey on the Oregon Trail. Nothing! We went home and he followed all instructions given. He was fine to go back to work on the following Monday. It really was no big deal!

Yes, I brought in a sample six weeks later. I wasn't going to risk it! Even that wasn't painful for Ron—maybe a little embarrassing, but no pain involved. Plus, I was the one who drove it down to the office and put my husband's "man-hood" on the counter and waited for the nurse to come back and give the "all clear." And, no, he never did go to the toe doctor. Miraculously, the pain in his toe disappeared! Come to think of it, Ron has never asked me to call the doctor for him since. Hmmmm.

Halleluiah! Now we knew that our family was complete. A month later, I gave birth to another beautiful baby boy— Caleb, which means "faithful." I love that name and its meaning. It's a reminder to me that God is faithful with His family planning. He knew that Ron and I were well-suited to handle a big gaggle of boys and that is what we got. When I say well-suited, I don't mean that we had the "means," we just had the grit. We lived in a three-bedroom house and were making it on one income, so we had neither the room nor the money to justify a growing family, but we were less focused on what we didn't have and much more in tune with what we did—which was each other.

Most of the stories in this book were not a bit funny at the time (except for the one about the Christmas tree and the car wash—THAT one was funny from the get-go), but looking back on them, they are ALL hilarious! Tragedy plus time equals comedy! I wrote this book for mothers and grandmothers because all moms occasionally say UGH!™ And they need to add some la la la la to their UGH and make it a laUGH!™

As you read my stories, I hope you laugh with me, at me, and at yourself because laughter makes life a lot more joyful!! And, I hope you will share this book with other moms who need a good laugh! As I wrote the book, I imagined moms reading it at soccer practices, on trains or buses as they commute to work, and of course, in bathrooms all over the world (a mom's only sanctuary). I imagined moms giving it and receiving it as a gift for holidays, birthdays, Mother's Day, baby showers, and especially as a "pick-me-up" when Mom has had her *cookies officially frosted* and she just needs to know that she is not alone! Enjoy!

And please go to my website and read the rest of the stories. I couldn't fit them all here. You have to read the "not me" story, and the one about my husband AND my son who were both taken to the ER within twelve hours of each other. And, you have to read about the time my two-year-old got in my mini-van and drove it down my driveway right into my neighbor's driveway across the street. I won't spoil the ending. You'll have to go to the site and see how that one turned out. It was VERY EXCITING! Oh, that reminds me that I also have the story of how I stopped saying "You kids are driving me NUTS!" But, again, I just couldn't get them all into one book. You can find me online at **www.tracydegraaf.com** and at **www.laughanywaymom.com**. I'm also on lots of social media sites like Facebook, Twitter, LinkedIn, etc... Find me there so we can keep the conversation going.

Chapter One

How to Become an Emergency Room
Frequent Flyer in 21 Visits or Less

To Stitch or Not to Stitch

Raising kids will definitely keep you in stitches. Kids are toUGH!™ Mine, at least, don't seem to do much of anything in a quiet and peaceful sort of way. My kids will head-butt, wrestle, and roughhouse until someone is crying or bleeding or both.

One day, I invited my friends over for a Mary Kay cosmetics party. My good friend, Kathy, was a Mary Kay Consultant and it had been awhile since I had done something like this (mostly because my youngest at the time wasn't quite a year old). It would be a real treat to have my gal pals over for some pampering—and NOT the diaper kind.

"BOOOOOOOYSSSSS, Get these Legos outta here!" I said for the eighteenth time. Trying to keep my house clean was like trying to keep up with Richard Simmons in Disneyland—impossible. But, I was determined to have a relaxing night with my friends and do so in a clean environment. The toys were shoved in the boys' bedrooms, and my living room carpet had fresh vacuum markings in the shape of Ws in the corners of the room. I even lit the two wall sconces I got from a Home Interiors party my friend Laurie had had the year before; and I had a jumbo "pumpkin spice" Yankee Candle pumpin' out the pumpkin scent throughout the house. Utopia!

My friends arrived and I put a peach cobbler in the oven so it would be ready when the facials were complete. There were eight women sitting around my kitchen table with our hair pulled back in headbands and a Styrofoam tray full of blobs of cleanser, mask, moisturizer, foundation, and a nicely saturated cotton ball of toner in front of each. It was time for us ladies to relax and enjoy.

My friend Susan brought her teenage daughter, Kara, to watch over my boys while we did our thing. Kara took them outside and Luke, our athletic one (age ten at the time), strapped on his Rollerblades. (Yes, he wore a helmet and knee and elbow pads.) They were out of the house for about five minutes when Kara came rushing back inside with a worried look on her face.

"Luke fell and he's bleeding," she said.

Sure enough—he split open his chin. It was the first time I had been faced with a cut deep enough to require stitches. I didn't even know what the "stitches criteria" were. How does one know when a Band-Aid isn't going to "cut" it? Another friend, Janet (a seasoned been-there-and-done-that mom), confirmed that it would definitely need a stitch or two, and she drove me and Luke to the closest ER. I sat in the backseat of Janet's Suburban and held a blood-stained washcloth on his chin while trying to keep both of us from freaking out—I hate medical stuff. Little did I know then that I would eventually make several trips to the ER with multiple children for a variety of reasons! It's true what they say. You do become numb to it—even when it's your own kid—because you know that it will eventually work out fine.

A few hours later, Janet and I returned home with "Luke-en-stein" and his five stitches and a small Lego set that I bribed him with in order to get him to sit still while the ER doc shot a needle full of painkiller right into the gaping hole in his face. (I almost puked!) When we walked into my house, my lady friends were all beautified by the Mary Kay consultant, and the peach cobbler had been served. Everyone went home, and I crawled in bed not feeling like I had pampered myself at all.

A few years passed before we had our second encounter with stitches. It also involved Luke and his chin. He was playing at a friend's house (a busy household with three boys), and they were creating makeshift ramps and jumping over stuff on skateboards. Luke bit the pavement with his chin and split open the very same spot he had two years earlier. He now has a permanent reminder of his youthful days of terror on wheels, and it's doubtful that he will ever look good with a goatee.

But it is our fourth son, Adam, our absolute daredevil, who proudly holds the record for the most stitches, both in number and in trips to the ER to get them. Of all our five boys, he is the boy-iest! He's the only one I've ever said "Don't put that in your mouth!!" when I saw him one day lying on his back in the grass with his arm outstretched holding up a dead mouse by the tail. Why did I think Adam might put the corpse of a mouse in his mouth? Let's just say that he is the type that would do it out of pure curiosity (or craziness) or if he was dared to (and for sure he would do it if he was dared NOT to).

I learned early on that if I was to survive mothering Adam, I was going to have to get tough and quick! His first ER trip was pretty basic. At the age of four, he slammed his own hand in the slider door of our minivan. We stopped to visit friends, and we barely got into the house when we heard a bloodcurdling scream. We still can't figure out exactly how he did it. When you think about it, it is darned near impossible to catch your own hand in the slider door of a minivan. But somehow, he found a way. I am hopeful that his determined character will contribute to his success someday. But on that day, it led to a half-dozen stitches in his finger. He got two Popsicles for being a good boy for the doctor.

His next ER visit, four years later, was not quite as simple. He got clocked in the head by a line drive while pitching in a friendly game of neighborhood baseball led by Cal, one of the dads on our street. By the way, this is the same neighbor whose driveway our van was parked in when Adam slammed his finger in the door—I see a pattern. I was at work when Cal called to tell me that I better come and take a look at Adam's head injury, because it may need a stitch or two. Cal was a police officer and his wife was a nurse, so I knew they could handle even the most chaotic situation. When I pulled into the driveway, the other boys had gone home and only

Cal was sitting on the front porch, with Adam lying on his lap with ice wrapped in a kitchen towel held on his head.

Adam started to whimper just a little when he saw me, and Cal told him that everything was going to be fine. Cal lifted the ice pack to reveal the wound, and I saw actual proof that there really are seven layers to human skin. I almost lost my lunch. I could see white stuff, and it looked like sliced chicken breast that I use in my stir-fry. Totally gross!

I gently took the ice pack and placed it back on Adam's head, swallowed hard and reclaimed my stomach. We got in the car to go to the ER. Cal offered to drive, but I assured him that I had done this before and that I could handle it on my own. It wasn't a big deal.

Adam required fourteen stitches in all, some on the inside and some on the outside. We had a nurse whose eight-year-old son happened to be a champion bull rider. So, I turned to the nurse and said, "Oh, so you've been through this with your kid, right?" To which he said, "NO, not a single stitch. They wear protective gear." Yes, the thought did cross my mind to ask him where I could get some of that gear, but I knew I could never get my kids to wear it anyway. So I might as well just settle in for the ride! If only my "ride" were eight seconds on a bull.

The third time that Adam required some patchwork came when he was about eight years old and it was an extremely cold February day in the Chicagoland area. It was twenty below with the windchill factored in (Chicagoans always tell you how cold it is by windchill. They don't call it the windy city for nothing.) Adam never let a little thing like weather stand in the way of him going outside. He didn't see a problem with bundling up and taking on the cold. It was a Saturday, and my husband and I refused to allow him to go outside and play; but we relented and did say yes to him going over to the next-door neighbor's house to play video games.

Out the door he flew, while my husband watched from the warmth of our dining room window with a hot cup of coffee in his hand. Halfway down our stone driveway, Adam hit a patch of ice and slipped. He fell forward and since he had his hands in his pockets (no gloves), his face took the brunt of the impact. Thank God he didn't bust a tooth! Ron saw the whole thing happen and rushed out to get him. He brought Adam inside and asked me if I could clean him up and put a "butterfly" bandage on it.

The kid's face looked like a pound of hamburger that had been dropped on a dirt road. There was blood everywhere with tiny bits of gravel mixed with dirt and snow shoved up in his mug.

"There was no way I can even get it all cleaned out, let alone figure out how to put his lips back together," I said.

I was afraid that if I patched him up, he would end up looking like Mick Jagger FOREVER. I couldn't risk it and said we have to let the professionals handle this.

When we got to the hospital, the doctor really gave us a hard time.

"It's very dangerous to be outside in this kind of cold. Children have no business being outside in sub zero temperatures," she said.

We knew that. He wasn't "playing" outside. He was supposed to be WALKING next door to play inside. But Adam doesn't WALK anywhere. He's an "all or nothing" type of kid—(sort of like a firecracker—it's either lit or it's not). And a lit firecracker is going to make some noise! He definitely lives each day to the fullest!

I can only hope that our "quilting" days are behind us. But, somehow, I wouldn't be surprised if we end up with another split-open chin, finger, or knee. We still have several years of skateboarding, football, and getting in and out of minivans left ahead. Time will tell!

Sticks and Stones Equal Broken Bones and NOW WHAT'S a Mom to Do?

"Hello."

"Mrs. DeGraaf?"

It was Jan, the secretary at the elementary school.

"Yes," I answered.

"Nate fell off a swing at recess, and we think you should come to the school and take a look at it," she said.

"How bad it is?" I asked.

"Well, we just think you should come and take a look," she said.

"Okay, I'll be right there."

Moments later, I arrived at the elementary school. Nate, my eldest son, was sitting in the office with his right arm sandwiched between a dictionary and a Ziploc bag filled with ice. He was in the fourth grade. His eyes were red from crying, and he looked scared to death.

I walked over to him and said, "Okay, let me see."

The kid raised his arm just enough for it to leave the support of the dictionary. His entire forearm slumped like a worn-out hammock between two young trees. It was clear to me that this needed more than Webster and Ziploc.

"Oh boy!" I sighed. "How did you do that?"

"I was on a swing and fell backward and put my arm back to break the fall," he said.

"You broke something all right!"

This was not the first time that I had seen a broken limb. The same kid broke his leg in a freak accident eight years earlier when he was only two by tripping over a chunk of concrete. I heard his bones crack upon impact and knew it was NOT GOOD. That time, he only fell twelve inches, but by dinner, he was knee-deep in a purple cast, in honor of his beloved "Barney the Dinosaur." He is now 6'3" with facial hair and has disavowed his affiliation with Barney like a slick politician throwing an old mistress under the bus. But, back in the day, Barney comforted Nate.

Not only did I know, firsthand, what a broken bone looked like and sounded like, I also knew what it felt like, since I snapped both my tibia and fibula clean through when I was ten. The pain was so intense that I was sure I would die because of it. I definitely had compassion in that moment in Jan's office of the elementary school. I saw fear in my son's eyes. I was wishing that he had just let himself fall completely off the swing instead of putting his arm back. Maybe that would have been less damaging. But, no such luck. I signed him and his brother Luke (age nine) out of school and made arrangements for my three little guys to stay with a neighbor while I drove Mr. "Fall a Foot and Break a Bone" to the doctor.

"Yes, it's broken and because of the nature of the fracture and because your son is still growing, I am going to send you to a bone specialist to have it set," our family doctor informed me. I asked for something to take the edge off a bit—and a dose of Tylenol for my son would be good too. Just kidding!

The bone specialist took more X-rays and confirmed the previous confirmation of, indeed, the bones were broken (which by the way, I had diagnosed back in the school when I saw the "hammock" thing, but what do I know, I am just a mother). The good news was that the break didn't require surgery, and the specialist could set it right there in the office. He was confident that my son would recover fully. Halleluiah!

Okay, that sounded good to me. The specialist explained that in order to set it, he would have to manipulate Nate's arm. There would be some pain involved, but it would last only for a moment. Then he would be cast and we could be on our way.

My mind instantly flashed back to 1975 and I could see my own childhood physician, Dr. Simonetta, tipping his chin down and peering at me over his thick black-rimmed glasses saying the same thing as he set my broken leg. Strangely, I remember him having an unusual amount of hair in his nostrils. Ummm. I had begged him not to cut my sister's NEW corduroy pants that I was wearing because she would KILL ME! Snip, Snip, Snip! The pants were shredded and somehow, Dr. Simonetta managed to set my leg while he distracted me with conversation. I don't remember the content of it other than my ignored protest about the pants; and, of course, I remember the nose hair.

"Okay, Nate, hold my hand, and let the doctor do what he has to do," I said. I will never forget the look of sheer betrayal that my son shot at me as he gripped my fingers with the strength of ten men and screamed "Mommy" while his bones were being realigned. It took my breath away. Luke was just sitting there, motionless, with his hands over his eyes and peeking through his fingers like he was watching *The Amityville Horror.*

"We will see you in two weeks for another set of X-rays to check on the healing progress. Give him Tylenol for pain, and keep his arm elevated for the next twenty-four hours," the nurse instructed. Finally, we were on our way home.

That wasn't the first or the last trip to a doctor's office for our lively bunch. To date, we have endured six bone fractures, five trips to the ER for stitches, three allergic reactions, one appendectomy, and one fever of 105 degrees. Oh, and I almost forgot about the times we went to the emergency room because my youngest kid shoved rocks up his nose and a few years later swallowed a coin. Read on …

How NOT to Remove a Foreign Object from Your Child's Nose!

"Caleb, don't you DARE take those shoes off again!" I said to my two-year-old who was strapped in his car seat squirming to be freed from the confines of his Spider Man tennis shoes. He hated wearing shoes and took advantage of every opportunity to kick them off. This totally drove me batty because it wasn't easy to get his chubby little feet into the shoes in the first place. My husband said it reminded him of his days as a senior in high school when he worked at a shoe store in the mall and the more "mature" women would politely ask for a size 7 when their feet were really a 9. They would always blame it on swelling from walking in the mall.

In spite of my careful loving instruction, he did it again! I could feel my son's legs hitting the back of my seat as we drove home from church on a beautiful Sunday afternoon. He was warned that I would make him walk in the house with just his socks on if he did it again, so be it!

Reasoning with a two-year-old is like trying to salvage burned toast—a complete waste of time. When we got into our driveway, which, at the time, was gravel (we were saving up for asphalt), I opened his door, unbuckled his car seat, and told him I was going inside to make lunch. He could join me whenever he felt ready. He sat down on the gravel driveway, folded his arms with an exaggerated shrug, and pushed out his lower lip.

I was content to let him deal with the consequences of his actions and I went inside. I was in the kitchen when a few minutes later, he was at my side.

"Mommy, owie," he whined, touching the side of his nose with his plump index finger.

I looked into his tiny nostril and could see a small rock up there. I hedged on whether or not I could get it myself with a pair of tweezers and decided (wisely) not to attempt retrieval on my own. I didn't want to shove it even farther into the dark holes of his head. So, I put his chubby little feet back into the shoes (*UGH!*™), strapped him back into the car seat, and assured my husband that it looked like no big deal. I would be fine taking him to the emergency room by myself. Ron stayed home with the rest of the team.

My son and I waited in the ER waiting area for an hour or so for the nurse to call us, and when we got into the examining room, I told the whole story to the doctor taking our case. She gently lifted my son's nostril and poked and prodded a little and removed the rock with ease. No problem. *See? All better*, I thought. The doctor put her special light back up his nose and said, "Oh boy." That was when I knew it was going to be a long day. There was another rock wedged way back in his nasal cavity that she couldn't reach. She tried to get it, but it was way up there. She told us to sit tight, and she would be right back.

A few moments later, another nurse came in and said we were going to move to a different room that was better equipped to "extract the foreign object." The first doctor we saw introduced us to another doctor (a little older). He was the head of the ER and would take over our case. He couldn't get it either! Where is Dr. Welby when you need him?

So, the second doctor called an ear, nose, and throat specialist to remove the rock. By the time he got there, my son was fighting this whole thing like a mad cat getting a flea bath! It took five adults to hold the kid down while the ENT doc worked on him. I was wishing I had sent my husband to handle the no-big-deal trip to the ER for the no-big deal-rock up the nose, and that I was home with "the rest of the team."

Finally, after about twenty-five minutes of digging into his nose with a curved pronged metal instrument, the ENT doc loosened the rock. It flung up into the air and landed smack-dab in Caleb's wide-open screaming mouth. OM-Gosh!! It got stuck in his throat and he started to choke. The medical staff flipped him over and blood from his nose went everywhere. "Oh dear Lord, somebody shoot me!" was my silent prayer.

They turned him upside-down and pounded on his back with a Heimlich move and alas, victory was ours! The ENT doc told me, "We were about thirty seconds away from taking him to surgery to remove that rock." What a day! I shed a few tears as I held my baby and calmed him after such a traumatic experience, and we proceeded to head back home.

My pooped-out two-year-old fell asleep in the car, and I pulled into the driveway feeling like I had just run the Iron Man TWICE, backward and on one leg. I was completely exhausted! I was greeted by my next two youngest sons, Joel and Adam (ages six and four). Joel had a grimaced look on his face as he showed me his hand with a huge splinter in it. Meanwhile, Adam sort of limped over to my car and said "Mom, I think I have glass in my foot." UGH!™

I couldn't believe it. I solicited the help of my husband to deal with these new injuries. I had taken care of the most critically wounded that day, and he could handle the first aid stuff! Then I took a well-deserved nap!

Does Swallowing a Nickel Make You a Vending Machine?

I was in the kitchen barking my usual inquiries, "Who made this mess? Who left the milk out? And who is going to clean this up?" (I swear; one of these days I am going to have the FBI come and dust my kitchen for prints and prove my point, once and for all, that "NOT ME" has a real identity!)

My kindergartner, Caleb, who was always into something, came rushing to me with an alarmed look on his face as he yanked on the tail end of my shirt and told me that he had just swallowed a quarter.

"WHAT were you doing with a quarter in your mouth?" I asked, STUNNED!

"I don't know," he cried. His eyes dropped and he

gestured to his throat. "It's stuck right here," he said.

Well, this was a new one for me. I didn't know if I should pound on his back, give him a glass of water, or kick him like a Coke machine. I decided to call the poison control center and get their take on the situation.

"Poison Control, how can we help you?" the voice answered.

"I think my five-year-old has a quarter stuck in his throat. Do you have any advice?"

"Can he talk okay and is he getting enough oxygen?" the voice inquired.

"Yes, he can talk and breathe fine, but he says he can feel it in his throat. Should I give him something to drink?"

"NO, you never want to do that because the object could move and he could actually choke on it. Take him to the nearest emergency room," the voice advised.

Oh great, another trip to the ER. We had been there so many times that I was certain that the social workers would investigate us for sure! This time, I took my husband with me because I had learned the hard way that there's no such thing as a "no-big-deal" trip to the ER and I wasn't going to the pokey alone! When we arrived, it was obvious that our little "vending machine" was a bit uncomfortable, but not completely OUT OF ORDER. A nurse led us to an available room and, as we walked down the familiar hallway, she turned to me and said, "Do I know you?"

"I've never see you before in my life," I said, hoping she wouldn't remember the eight times we had been there in the previous fifteen months. I did, however, recognize the nurse who took care of us during one of our many trips to the ER for stitches. I remembered him because he was the one who had an eight-year-old son who participated in rodeos. I quickly ducked into the examination room.

He followed us in and said, "You're back! What happened this time?" My husband told him that our boy apparently missed the slot of his piggy bank and now he had a quarter stuck in his throat. "Boys will be boys," the nurse said. He knew that we had five of them, and we weren't questioned any longer. It felt like being automatically excused from jury duty. I must say that I sort of liked that feeling!

Moments later, a nurse and a security guard came into the room. Great! We are going to jail, I thought. They instructed my son to stand up and the nurse said, "Scan 'em." The security guard held his metal detection scanning wand close to my son's head and moved it slowly downward. BEEP, BEEP, BEEP, BEEP it went off just below his chin.

"Ok," the nurse said, "Get him undressed and put this gown on him and let's go down to X-ray for a picture."

The security guard grinned and whispered, "Looks like you're busted, kiddo."

Our son had started to drool because his saliva was sort of "dammed" off by the quarter, so we gave him a drool bib and put a little hospital gown on him. (Yes, even the little kid gowns are open in the back. But unlike an adult, he couldn't care less about showing the world his Scooby Doos!)

The X-rays showed that indeed the "foreign object" was lodged in his throat. We saw a perfectly round coin smack dab in the middle of his esophagus. His breathing was fine, but he was becoming more frustrated with the discomfort and his drool bib needed to be replaced with a drool bowl because the kid was definitely leaking!

Of course, it was late on a Sunday night, and they had to call an ear, nose, and throat doctor to come and take the case. I prayed that we would not get the same guy who dug the rock out of Caleb's nose a few years prior—not because I had a problem with the doctor, but just the embarrassment of being back yet again with yet another "UFO" lodged in another orifice of my kid's head was more than I could take.

The nurse explained that the coin would have to be removed by a surgeon and that they would need to use general anesthesia to knock Caleb out and go in through his mouth with a special tool and suction the coin to remove it. There was a chance that the procedure would force the coin down and if that were the case, then it would likely go into his stomach and follow the Taco Bell he had for lunch out the back door via the "Scooby Doo" route. We would then have to "find" it or come back in for a follow-up X-ray to be sure it had passed.

Either option sounded unpleasant, but what else could we do? The nurse gave me the consent forms for surgery and asked if anyone in the family has had an allergic reaction to anesthesia. I started to fill out the paperwork. In the back of my mind, I thought that my husband's grandmother had a problem with a drug reaction during a surgery, so I asked if I could call my mother-in-law to check.

Meanwhile, the surgeon was on his way, and my husband had Caleb on his lap with the drool bowl. While I was on the phone, my husband noticed a change in our son's disposition. He stopped whining and the drooling shut down too.

"Hey, Trace, I think it went down," Ron said.

"I feel better. Let's go home," Caleb said.

"Hold on partner," said the nurse as she picked up the phone and once again paged security.

The guard came and held his wand over Caleb's stomach and BEEP BEEP BEEP BEEP the metal detector went off. Yes, the coin had been safely deposited into his tummy. A second X-ray confirmed this and the ER staff signed us out with instructions to make sure it passed by "checking" through his YOU KNOW WHAT.

Great! At least he didn't have to go through surgery and have it sucked out of his mouth. I guess I could endure a little "quarter hunting."

Well, I searched through quite a few specimens, and never did find that quarter. I am pretty sure it ended up at a local McDonald's. A few days following this whole ordeal, my sister, Kelli, and I took all of our kids to eat at McDonald's and Caleb, who was playing in the indoor play place, raced past us to the restrooms and yelling, "I have to poooooop" really loud. The other patrons of the restaurant smiled and chuckled as I crawled under the table and Kelli and my niece laughed hysterically. I refused to look for that quarter in a public restroom. Ronald McDonald could KEEP THE CHANGE!

Emergency Room Survival Tips

1. Have printed directions to the nearest ER in your car along with surrounding ERs as well. Depending on insurance, and depending on why you need to go there, you may find (like we did) that you have a favorite ER. Even though there are closer hospitals to our home, we will take the boys to St. Mary's for nonlife threatening "emergencies" because it's not as crowded, the staff is nicer, and they know us by first name.

2. Keep Tylenol in your purse—just in case. It can take hours to get a dose of Tylenol from a nurse in the Emergency Room. If you really need it, and they say it is okay to take it, but it's been four hours since you made your request, it's nice to have in your purse!

3. Keep quarters and dollar bills in your purse for the vending machines. (Keep all coins AWAY from small children!)

4. Bring something to read and an Ipod or video game for your kid.

5. Make someone go with you. There is no such thing as a "no-big-deal" trip to the ER.

6. Have information about any allergic reactions to anesthesia medication handy.

7. Have your family doctor and immediate family contact information handy.

8. Use your own pen for signing papers. Don't touch the one provided. There are sick people in the hospital. If you walk in there without a problem, you may walk out with one.

9. Wash your hands, use hand sanitizer for reasons listed above.

10. Don't be afraid to ASK for something you need. I once spent eight hours in an Emergency Room (not St. Mary's) with my three-year-old, Caleb, who had a fever of 105 degrees. He was hooked up to an IV bag on a bed that was set up in what looked like a storage room (the hospital was overcrowded and it was after this trip that we started shopping around for better ERs).

There was NO CHAIR in the room and I had to stand next to the bedside for eight hours. Four or five different doctors and nurses came in and out of the room during the course of the day and none offered to get me a chair. Caleb fell asleep and I finally sat down on the cold tile floor. A short Hispanic woman dressed in what looked like a housekeeping uniform came in and asked, "How is he doing?" "He's asleep now," I said, "but he sure didn't like getting that IV." She smiled and said, "I hope he feels better soon." She left the room only to return a moment later with a chair for me. "Here," she said, "you'll be more comfortable." I was so thankful for her gracious gesture and I found myself puzzled at why one of the others didn't do the same. Of all the people we encountered that day, the woman from housekeeping was likely the one receiving the least in pay and she probably didn't have a college degree. Yet, she was the one who showed us the most compassion and common sense. Next time, I will just ASK the first person I see for whatever I need.

Chapter Two

Gal Pal Chats by the Fireside

How a Large Yellow Bus Saves My Sanity at 7:21 a.m.

On school days, "the big yellow savior" comes to my house twice since my five boys attend different buildings in our district. I usually greet our bus driver, Miss Marti, on the first day back to school with some sort of appreciative "reward." It's a ceremonial passing of the baton that brings tears to both of our eyes, albeit with different emotions behind them.

Our neighborhood is in the middle of nowhere, and surrounded by corn and bean fields, so I can look out my kitchen window and see the bus when it's still a quarter mile down the road. When I spot the streak of yellow and black heading our way, I yell "BUS" as loud as I can and the two youngest of my boys (Adam and Caleb) have about sixty seconds to grab their shoes, lunch, and backpack and get to the end of our very long driveway. I've decided not to encourage either of them to pursue careers as firefighters because I'm sure they would leave some essential piece of equipment (like the water hose) behind. It never fails that I come across last night's homework or this week's library book right when I hear the diesel engine of that bus pulling away from my street.

One time I decided to color my roots in the midst of this morning craziness, and wouldn't you know, that was the day Miss Marti wanted to talk to me about my kid and those darned ants in his pants.

I stood at my front door in my Winnie the Pooh slippers, flannel pajamas, and my faded '85 Bears Super Bowl T-shirt (no bra, of course), hoping that the bus driver's wave was just a friendly gesture and not a requisition. I stood corrected as the bus ceased to move while Miss Marti's arm waved with a vengeance out the driver's side window. Oh well, I thought, as I grabbed my husband's John Deere jacket and out to the bus I trotted with my Phyllis-Diller-gone-

Elizabeth-Taylor-looking hairdo. Talk about scaring school-children! UGH!™

"What's up?" I asked, pretending that I didn't look like a five-foot-seven-inch sea otter who had survived the *Exxon Valdez* oil spill.

She looked down at me from atop her elevated vantage point and said, "Nice hair."

I grabbed the edges of my husband's jacket and wrapped it across my chest to hide the fact that my "girls" were going along for the ride unbuckled.

"I had to move Adam to the seat right behind me for now. I just wanted you to know," Marti said. She was always fair, and I loved that she didn't put up with any shenanigans on her bus!

"Okay, no problem," I agreed. "What was he doing?"

"Well, I can't tell who started what, but he and another boy were apparently pulling the hair clips out of some girl's hair, and it went from there. I moved both of the boys, and we will just keep an eye on things."

"Okay, just let me know if you continue to have a problem," I said. "BE GOOD BOYS," I yelled while pointing at them behind Marti's head. As the bus pulled away, I could see the mystified faces of a few girls in the back window as they strained their necks to get one more look at me. I'm sure they thought they had just seen a real-life vampire with the fashion sense of an unemployed clown.

I am convinced that bus drivers have a special place in heaven, (along with mothers of five boys) and their retirement packages should include a two-week-all-expense-paid trip to Hawaii!

The Do-It-Yourself Way to Raising Kids Who Actually Do

"I'm hungry," my young blond-haired seven-year-old said with intention.

"Hello Hungry, I'm Mom," I said.

Caleb was not amused. He obviously wanted me to end his one-man famine and make something for breakfast. On mornings-gone-by, before I became completely overwhelmed with five kids, I would have jumped right up, dropped whatever I was doing, and made the boy a decent breakfast. But, I am older and wiser than a decade ago, so I told him that he was perfectly able and welcome to decide what he wanted to eat, make it, and eat it. (By the way, I would have never said that to my firstborn when he was that age. I didn't know that seven-year-olds could use a knife until AFTER I had more than three kids!)

"But, Mom, you're closer to the freezer," Caleb said.

I knew he wanted waffles. I had just been to the grocery store, and we had a huge box of three dozen waffles right there in the freezer, which, as he so conveniently observed, I was closest to.

"Yes, I know that, but I am one person, and there are seven people living in this house. So if I make everyone's breakfast, I'll be popping waffles into the toaster until next Tuesday."

Caleb got out the waffles and the sugar-free maple syrup (sugar makes him shoot off like a Roman candle, so we avoid it), and he made his own breakfast. But, men don't give up that easily. He tried again.

"Mom, will you cut these?" he requested, while holding his plate of syrup-drenched waffles toward me.

I told him that he was perfectly able and welcome to get a knife and cut his waffles and eat them. He walked away, only slightly defeated, and stood next to his chair at the kitchen table. With a fork held tightly in his left hand, he held down the pair of waffles and started to cut large uneven pieces with the knife in his right. He struggled with the plastic plate moving around the table a bit, but he eventually got it. That was the end of the battle. It was a hard-fought mental war, but I felt the nod went to Mom on that one.

Later in the day, I asked my sixteen-year-old son, Luke, to clean the pool filter, (about a twenty-minute job). It involved shutting off valves, opening up the filter, rinsing off components, and replacing everything. It wasn't rocket science, but it did require some effort. He had done it before, and I was sure that he was quite competent to complete the task.

Luke followed me out to our backyard pool and I helped him get started. I no sooner got back into the house and the back door flung open.

"MOM, I can't figure it out," Luke shouted.

I walked him back outside and started to unscrew the various parts of the filter so that it could be hosed off. I closed the intake valve and opened the outflow one (always a pain for me because my husband gives everything he tightens an extra ounce of Popeye). It felt like it was at least ninety degrees out that day. I was sweating like a marathon runner wearing a snowsuit. As I carefully explained the steps involved in disassembling the unit, I glanced at Luke and noticed that he was fiercely chewing on a fingernail and then examining his handiwork. He wasn't even paying attention!

And then the lightbulb went on. I stopped what I was doing, shook my head with my eyes squinted slightly and lips forming a sly grin. "Ah HA!" I said to my beloved son. "I've got you figured out. You want me to THINK that you can't do this task so that I will just do it for you. Well, cowboy, I've seen you disassemble and reassemble a paintball gun in two minutes flat, so this filter right here is your project and by golly, you will figure it out. Your little routine of 'roll over and play dumb' is not going to work with this savvy mother, so forget about it!"

And, in the end, he did, and I felt that I made great strides in ensuring my survival with my arms barely over my the life ring as I bob about in my testosterocean that I call HOME! A smart mama combined with a little self-sufficiency makes Luke a good boy and a fine catch for some lucky young lady someday.

If Father Knows Best, Why Do Kids Always Ask Mom First?

Before my boys could talk, I couldn't wait for them to say "Mama." All five of them said "Dada" first, which totally ticked me off. Now, they say, "Mom, Mommy, Maaaaaaaaam, Hey Mom, Where's Mom, I'm telling Mom," **CONSTANTLY**. It never ends. They rarely, if ever, go to Dad with a request for information. The only time I heard them say "Dad" was when it was followed by "did you fart?"

I was at Target once getting school supplies for the boys when my cell phone rang.

"Mom?"

It was Joel, who was entering junior high.

"No, it's Hillary Clinton. Who did you think you were calling?"

"Make sure you get me a green folder with pockets but no clasps. Okay?"

"Okay."

"Bye."

I moved my cart two feet (had to kick a few discarded Hello Kitty backpacks out of the way) and the phone rang again.

"Oh, and Mom?"

"No, still Hillary and what did Bill do this time?"

"Mom, you're not even funny. Just make sure you get me green. It has to match my spiral. The teacher said. Okay?"

"I got it. Green, pockets, no clasp."

I moved another two feet and picked up two Incredible Hulk hot/cold Thermos containers, thinking *my youngest boys will love these.*

My cell phone chimed yet again.

"Mom, when are you going to be home? I can't find the pink eraser you bought me."

"At this rate, I'll be home when you're ready to leave for college. Where is Dad?"

"He's on the couch watching the game."

"Ok, listen to me very carefully. Your father is a responsible card-carrying member of the local 150 Operating Engineers. He can get a foundation to within a quarter-inch of grade by eyeballing it, and to top that, he still holds the record for longest wheelie in the Longwood Neighborhood of Naperville, Illinois. I think he can handle helping you prepare yourself for school tomorrow. I can be trusted to bring home a green folder with pockets and no clasp and will place it carefully in your backpack when I get home. DO NOT CALL ME AGAIN!!"

It drives me crazy when my children call me on my cell phone with my husband, also their parent, planted two feet from them on the couch. But they're men, so they know that he's there, but not really. His body is there, but his mind is in New York, where the Sox are beating the Yanks 4-2 in the bottom of the eighth.

I could be on an important phone call while stirring a vat of homemade chili and my husband could be lying on the sectional with a chilled glassful of Sun tea in one hand and the remote control in the other, casually flipping from channel to channel, and my sons would come to me to find out what year the Alamo was fought. It infuriates me!

I know that I am not the only one. I have observed other wives and mothers with the same frustration. I laugh to myself when in public and I hear only one side of a cell phone conversation, "Go ask your father!" or "I don't know, put your dad on the phone." Or my favorite, "Did I get a divorce and not know it? The last time I checked, you have a father, go ask him!"

Let's face it, most men struggle with commitment (a.k.a. making a decision). It doesn't matter if it's marriage, deciding on a restaurant, or giving a kid permission to go sledding without snow pants—it's not easy for men to take care of these things. Kids are geniuses. They do what works, so if they go to Dad for information and he grunts, scratches his belly and says, "Ask your mother," the little genius children will eventually cut out the middle man with his grunting and scratching, and go directly to Mom every time. That is why they will call Mom, even though she may be twenty-five miles from home on a multitasking expedition of school supply shopping, while Dad is seated comfortably just inches away on the couch. She is the kid's best bet for an actual answer. I wonder if they would ignore me if I sat on the couch holding the remote with a glazed-over look. Hmmm.

Can You Make My Varicose Veins into a Mermaid Tattoo?

How did I end up living with six guys? Back in the "day," my self-image would have eaten up such male affection, but I couldn't even keep a prom date. Jack Burns came down with a sudden "illness" two days before the dance and was miraculously cured the day after. Hmmmm.

Now, here I am 24/7/365, and men are coming out of the woodwork. The only problem, of course, is that five of them refer to me as "MOM" and they aren't concerned in the least with boosting my sense of self. They like to call me over to the TV to see the before and after shots of the mother of three who is now sporting a scant bikini and is back to her prepregnancy weight of a whopping ninety-eight pounds. She, of course, is a size 2. The only number 2 I've ever put on my hips came out of a drive-thru window!

My dad always said I had Aunt Veronica's big bones. I never met Aunt Veronica, but if I had, I don't suspect it would have made me feel any better. Right around the tender age of thirteen, I had a growth spurt. In what felt like a two-week pubescent interlude, my body went from a girl's size 10 to a lady's size 12. I have never broken free of the double digits since. *UGH!*™

I used to place culpability on my children for the loss of my figure. Let's face it, with five pregnancies (all of which went a week or two overdue), that's well over two hundred weeks of being with child, plus nursing and all that goes with that—blah blah blah. Between the cellulite, the varicose veins, and the stretch marks, why worry about what a few extra pounds does to my swimsuit image? I don't think *Sports Illustrated* has my number, and it seems to be a moot point anyway.

One time I went to a dermatologist to see what could be done about my varicose veins. She told me I could have them taken care of with a few injections, a pair of stockings the thickness of a banana peel, and a down payment of 600 bucks (considered cosmetic and not a legitimate medical expense so NOT COVERED by my insurance).

I had recently priced out pool slides for our above-ground pool, and I decided to spend the cash on the slide instead. It would provide me with a much higher measure of mental stability since the entertainment value for my boys would be greater than that of the absence of my varicose veins (which, by the way, they could not care less about— although, when they were still babies, they used to touch them and say "Mommy, owie?") Besides, I am pretty sure that for fifty bucks or so, a decent tattoo artist could connect the dots and create a nice-looking mermaid on my thigh.

My boys tell me I don't have to lose weight, but that's only when I catch them chowing down on one of my Weight Watchers frozen treats. "But, Mom, you're the most beautiful woman in the world. You don't need these 'diet' foods. You don't need to lose weight." Chomp. Chomp. Chomp.

My husband, God bless him, has never crossed the line that was drawn in the sand early in our nearly two-decade marriage. I've threatened to leave him to raise these boys by himself if he ever says yes to my incessant question, "Does my butt look big in these pants?" His answer has always been no answer at all, just a wily grin with a hug and, "Hon, you look awesome!" I married a genius.

While getting fitted for my new bifocals, the woman who works at my eye doctor's office pointed out that I have a very tiny nose bridge. She had a hard time finding a frame that would accommodate my extra-small bridge.

"Well, God Bless America," I said. "Of all the things I've wanted to be smaller on my body: my hips, my bottom, my feet, my chubby cheeks, my ears, my arms, my thighs…and the one thing on my anatomy that is referred to as "petite" is right between my eyes." I have to look in the mirror cross-eyed just to see it—unimpressive. Just my luck!

Well, just like the rest of the American public (other than the size 2 young lady on TV), I have attempted numerous approaches to weight loss. My personal favorite is the group meetings in the Weight Watchers program. I've made a lot of friends there. I went to a meeting once and was highly praised because I lost six ounces. I even got a star sticker for my bookmark. It was a good thing I peed before the meeting, or I would have missed out on that rounding applause and affirmation!

Just about the time I decided to be "okay" with my bumps and curves, Angelina Jolie started pumping out kids like a PlayDoh fun factory. How does she do it? Her arms look like pencils. Mine have the girth of Rosie the Riveter minus the muscle! When can we go back to the Renaissance period when it was considered fashionable and a sign of wealth to be on the plump side? Plus, they had those really cool dresses that would collect all the "fat" north of a women's belly button and push it out the bra. Who said Pamela Anderson had anything up on fourteenth-century women?!

Mother of Five Retires From Haircuts at Home. UGH!™

Like most big families, we have found ways to cut corners and stretch a buck. I have saved money over the years by doing haircuts at home. It started out innocently enough when I attempted to give our two oldest boys, Nate and Luke (ages four and five at the time), skater cuts. They ended up with buzz cuts instead!

Hey, I tried.

They didn't seem to mind and actually liked their easy-breezy low-maintenance dos! A bonus was that it took months to grow out, which meant that we didn't have to worry about it for quite a while.

As soon as our boys reached the age of awakening (high school), they suddenly started to care about what their heads looked like. I think it had something to do with noticing girls because at about the same time, they would take a shower and brush their teeth without provocation. Amazing what hormones can do! That was when they "fired" me for their haircutting needs.

My oldest son, Nate, started going to the barber with my husband. His sideburns have never looked so good! Son #2, Luke, went to my stylist, who did wonders with his curly hair. She actually straightened it and showed him how to blow it dry so that it wasn't a nest of wild curls on the top of his head. I had always wondered why professional barbers and hairstylists were licensed, and now I know. It is because they actually know what they are doing!

One time, I crossed the line of no return and prematurely ended my "off the cuff" career as a hairdresser. I threw out all of my haircutting supplies—including the buzz cutter. My youngest boys were spared the embarrassment and character-building experience of wearing a knit cap to school in early September.

My "retirement" followed a disastrous haircut for son Joel (eleven and entering junior high just two days prior to the butchering of his tresses). He begged me to "trim" his hair, which had grown for several months to a very "Jonas Brothers-looking, I'm So Cool" length. Joel liked to whip his head quickly to the side in a smooth gesture to get his bangs out of his face. If you asked me, it looked like he was doing a shampoo commercial. His brothers called him the "Breck Girl." They had no real idea what they were talking about since they weren't around when the Breck girl commercials were on TV, but they had heard news reports that presidential candidate, John Edwards, spent several hundred dollars on a haircut, and some in the media were referring to him as "the Breck Girl." It caught on with the DeGraaf brothers—any reason to tease a brother is a valid reason.

So, with two days until school started, I decided to "trim" it. I started out okay, but something strange happened, and it was like I couldn't stop until it was too late.

Joel wanted the bangs a little shorter and I even said, "Let's take off just a little at a time. We can always cut more, but we can't put it back once it's cut."

Ten minutes later, I felt myself going farther and farther in the "hole" as Joel's head began to shrink into his neck. He held his body still and watched the long blond locks fall like the seeds off of cottonweed on a windy day.

Joel glanced up at me and said, "Mom, NOT TOO SHORT!!!"

I told him I was doing my best and that I wasn't a professional. I was trying to get the sides even and every time I would cut one side, the other would look shorter. Then I would cut more off of that side and the other one would look shorter still. It was madness!

When I finally stopped cutting, Joel took one look in the mirror, and the tears came. I felt terrible! Here is my young boy, about to enter the "junior high jungle of bloodsucking bullies," and I have just made him look like the biggest dork on the block!

Somebody shoot me!

I told him to go take a shower and maybe it will look better when he gets out. It didn't. He put on a hoodie and went to bed crying. He told me that I could homeschool him until Christmas because that was when he would go back to school!

In desperation, I offered him a bribe. "Would twenty bucks make you feel better?" I asked. Joel had been saving for an XBox 360. I thought that a twenty-dollar boost might help him forget about his botched haircut.

Joel's deep blue eyes were barely recognizable—they were so bloodshot. He looked at me and nodded that the twenty dollars would help. He stopped crying for a moment and said, "Mom, if I need surgery someday, are you going to try and save money and do that yourself too?"

"Of course not, Joel," I said as I offered him another twenty bucks. *UGH!*™

The next day, I was able to get him in to my hairstylist and she (a wonderful mom of three grown children) really helped sooth the sting of his short hair. She told him that she would just straighten it out. "It will all come in even and look nice—like the Jonas Brothers," she said.

That was all he needed (my forty bucks didn't hurt either). Joel had the strength to face the world of junior high, even with a Bill Gates haircut!

Sanity Survival Tips

1. **Put yourself first!** It sounds counterintuitive to a lot of mothers, but, trust me, there is a reason you are told to "secure your own oxygen mask." Obviously, if Mom loses herself in the process of mothering, who will be left to cut the crust off the bread? Keep yourself on your priority list!

2. **If you are married, put your marriage second!** Again, not a popular notion in our child-centered culture, but marriage is like taking care of houseplants. If you ignore them, well, you know the rest.

3. **Have a sense of humor!** Taking life too seriously has been known to lead to a bad case of the grumpies. Did you know that it is impossible to laugh and hold an angry thought at the same time? Look it up! It's a fact.

4. **Why not *shower* your family with prayer?** For me, having five sons is like juggling flaming swords. I have found the pathway to peace, and it's with daily prayer of thanks to God for one redeeming quality of each of my boys (sometimes a very short list) along with a daily request for an item of concern for each of my sons (sometimes a very long list). I sometimes incorporate this prayer time easily in the shower. I take a shower every day, so I pray for my boys every day. I smell good and my stress level is not so bad. It's a win-win.

5. **Embrace the differences!** Kids are all different. It amazes me how five people from the same two parents can be SO different! Someone actually asked me once if all my kids are from the same man. (I thought that was an odd question, but if I didn't KNOW that they are all mine and my husband's kids, I would have some questions based on personality differences. I have learned to embrace the fact that they are individuals.

6. **Balance your life!** Wow! It's hard enough to balance the checkbook, let alone an entire life. Let's just say "strive for balance in life." Get enough rest, enough exercise, enough sex, enough mental stimulation, enough conversation, enough challenge, enough fruits and veggies, enough water, enough vitamins, and especially

enough laughter. Enough means not too little and not too much. It means keeping margin on the page. Could you imagine reading this book if it had no margins? Talk about stressful! Our lives need white space. Just like our eyes need white space so they can rest while dancing from left to right across the pages of a book, we need to provide space in our lives so that we can breathe and have balance. Moms are especially guilty of trying to cram ten pounds of LIFE into a five pound bag. Balance, balance, balance!!!

7. **Be a student and major in boy!** Now this one is for all the moms out there with a son in your life. After my fifth boy came along, it was "Remember the Alamo, Baby." I knew that I was surrounded and completely outnumbered. I was living with six males. My only hope was to become a student of my "adversary." Understanding came as I read books about boys. *Wild at Heart* by John Eldridge was one of my favorites. That book helped me understand why my sons loved to roll around in the ditch in front of our house. It helped me to understand why my boys NEED to wrestle and snap each other with the wet end of a rolled-up towel.

8. **Give yourself a break!** Women are hard on themselves. Moms can be brutal at self-sabotage. Every once in awhile, give yourself permission to say, "This mom gig stinks to high heaven." Then go out to a chick flick with a few gal pals and you're good.

9. **Lower your standards!** Here in America, the land of opportunity, we STRIVE, STRIVE, STRIVE. Work hard and you'll succeed. I have no problem with that, but my advice to moms is to have realistic expectations of your limitations. Your kids have limits. You have limits. Your marriage has limits. So what if the boy shows up at school with two different shoes. Let It Go!

10. **Make a small change!** When my boys would be fighting or running through the house with scissors, or shooting Nerf bullets at the ceiling fan, I would yell really loud "You kids are driving me nuts!!!" Several times a day, I would hear myself saying that, so I tried to replace only the words. I kept the tone and the energy level the same and replaced the words with "This is very exciting!!" It was true—it was VERY EXCITING! My kids and I cracked up when I would say that. It just helped to diffuse the moment. It was a small change, but had a big impact.

Chapter Three

After All Charlie Brown, Isn't That What Christmas Is All About?

The DeGraaf Classic Christmas Tree-in-the-Car-Wash Story

Being a mother of five sons is akin to being a Coast Guard cutter commander on high alert. You never know when you may have to spring into action to assist in a rescue or ward off a surprise attack. The potential for a "boy venture" lurks around every corner. We've experienced rocks up the nose, fires in the oven, and frustration with wet cement; but there is one DeGraaf story that has become known as "The Classic." This is the one that friends will pull me aside after church to meet their sister from Cleveland and say, "Tell her the Christmas tree story—that's my favorite!"

So, here goes ...

It was a sunny mid-December Saturday and a temperate forty-five degrees in the Chicagoland area. The weather was perfect for taking the kids to the local tree farm to chop down our Christmas tree, as was our tradition. We piled our five boys in the minivan and headed out to the "U Cut Christmas Tree Farm," which was not too far from our home. Our oldest son was in junior high at the time and our youngest was about a year old.

The farm was teeming with people—lots of families out enjoying the warm spell before settling back into a typical Chicago winter. We spent a few hours wandering the fields in hunt of just the right tree (like it mattered). My most pressing concern was to be sure that the tree would actually fit in our living room. I didn't want to have to relocate the sectional to the garage next to the lawn mower while we spent the Christmas season sitting on the floor admiring a massive evergreen. When we finally all agreed on THE ONE, my husband chopped it down, while our older boys held onto it and two of the little guys lay on their bellies to watch. I held the baby, the camera, and six coats.

"Let's hop on the hayride so we don't have to walk back to the barn," I suggested. I didn't mention that my arms were numb from carrying all the gear. Ron marked our tree and put it in the bucket of the tractor while I got the kids situated on the bed of the hay wagon.

Back at the barn, we handed our tree to a man who put it on a shaker, bound it in plastic netting, and firmly secured it with twine to the luggage rack of our minivan. Even though we weren't cold, we drank some hot chocolate for nostalgia's sake and called it a day. Norman Rockwell couldn't have planned it better.

We decided to top off our "Rockwellian" afternoon by taking the boys to Pizza Hut. This was our first attempt at taking all five of them out to eat in public at the same time. Our fears were realized. It was pandemonium. Our littlest guy was extremely tired and fussy and our three-year-old (much to our server's dismay) spilled his drink. The other three boys were not really misbehaving, but they weren't exactly following the Emily Post rules of etiquette either.

By the time we were done, the boys had managed to get pizza sauce everywhere and our table looked like a bloody scene from _Rambo_. I am fairly certain that the expression on my face was beginning to look Rambo-ish too. Ron and I gathered up our boys and what was left of our sanity. We got back in the van, and headed home.

Although the suburban area that we live in is less than a forty-five-minute trip by car to downtown Chicago, our house is actually situated in a much more rural setting out in the country on a couple of acres. We are surrounded by gravel roads, so our vehicles are oftentimes covered with a white-grayish layer of dust. This is especially true in the winter when salt trucks are in abundance and the residue from the salt gets all over our cars as well. We have a habit of running our vehicles through the carwash just about every time we are in town because they get so dirty.

Someone at the Christmas tree farm had used his or her finger to write WASH ME on my rear window. Since it was such an unseasonably warm day, and since I had purchased fifty coupons at the local automatic car wash, and since I was in the habit of running the van through every time I was in town, and since it seemed like last week that we were at the Christmas tree farm instead of three hours ago.....

You guessed it......I turned to Ron and said, "Hey, babe, it's a beautiful day, let's get the car washed." Turns out, he is just as dumb as I am and he said, "Okay."

The carwash was jam-packed with people (remember it was December and forty-five degrees in Chicago—everyone was out getting the winter sludge off their vehicles). Every bay was full, and there were several people vacuuming out the inside of their cars and others towel drying. We got in line at the automatic behind two or three other cars. Someone else pulled in behind us, and we were just waiting our turn. Our vehicle, although stopped and in park, was swaying slightly as the boys bounced around in the backseat. It must have been quite a sight, our black minivan coated with grayish-white dust, swaying to and fro with our carefully selected neatly bound Christmas tree tied to the top awaiting its execution! *UGH!*™

We sat and waited for several minutes. A young man (looked like he was in his early twenties) came walking over to the driver's side window. Although I didn't recognize him, I thought Ron knew him from work or something, 'cause the guy had a big grin on his face.

The guy said, "Hey, man, how ya doin?"

"Pretty good," Ron said.

"You know you can't go in there," he said as he glanced up and pointed to the Christmas tree on the top of our van. He looked embarrassed FOR us.

At first, Ron looked at him with his head tilted slightly like a befuddled Cocker Spaniel while two deep folds formed between his eyebrows.

"Why not?"

And then reality set in for the both of us. We were about to go through the automatic pressure wash with an eight-foot Blue Spruce strapped to the roof of our vehicle. Ron looked at the guy and sheepishly said, "Oh, WOW, that's right. Thanks." Then he did a three-point tire-screeching turn to get the heck out of there as fast as possible! I am sure that the people behind us were upset that they didn't get to see our Christmas tree go through the rinse cycle! I have often wondered if any of the other bystanders would have stopped us from going in if the other guy hadn't given us a heads-up. I laughed so hard I was crying! I mean, I laughed all the way home and seriously almost wet myself.

In hindsight, I wish I had been a quick thinker and told the guy that we knew exactly what we were doing and that our kids have allergies so we have to wash the tree really well or our kids swell up like the Michelin Man. Perhaps he would have been impressed with our ingenuity. Instead, I'm sure he just felt sorry for our boys and the genetic pool from which they came. Our eldest son said he was going to write an essay titled, "Why My Parents Are Morons."

After Christmas that year, we bought an artificial tree—75 percent off, with the lights already attached. Now that I think about it, the carwash may be a viable option for cleaning that tree! It is kind of dusty. Perhaps we were just ahead of our time.

Black Friday Meets My In-Laws

My in-laws have Christmas shopping down to a science. I call them Blackfriologists. They are part of an underground secret social order that situate themselves like Daniel Boone lying in wait for his next kill in mall parking lots all over the country on the day after Thanksgiving (aka Black Friday). The only difference is that they are hunting for bargains instead of buffalo! They purchase dozens of Christmas gifts for every person on their list, including Sunday school teachers, coffee shop baristas, dog walkers, and chimney sweeps, all before dawn and for about a third of the regular cost.

They study the Black Friday websites for weeks prior to "the BIG day" and require that all the grandkids and nieces and nephews submit their wish lists before 11:59 p.m. on Turkey Day. They have been shopping this way for years and always invite me to come along. I graciously decline, not wishing to go anywhere near the crowds, not to mention the traffic on the busiest shopping day of the year. (Truth be told, I think they are nuts!) But, I went with them one year and was bowled over with shock and awe.

"Where are you?" my mother-in-law, Claudia, radioed to Kelly and Jaime, my two sisters-in-law.

"We are at Toys R Us waiting for it to open. Where are you guys?" Jaime said.

"We'll be heading your way as soon as we get out of Kohl's. Is it jam-packed there?" Claudia asked while checking her watch.

"Yeah. I would say there are about fifty people in line outside with others in their cars staying warm. What about you?" Jaime said.

"There're a handful of people here but not as many as last year. The cold probably kept some of them away," Claudia said. I was amazed that so many people cared so much about saving money that they would line up in the freezing cold to spend it. Hmmmm.

It was 4:35 a.m., pitch black outside, and about two degrees. We had hot coffee in travel mugs, comfortable shoes, "The Lists," and a map—not a street map, but a store map. We split up into pairs and divided the lists according to stores. While Claudia and I were at Kohl's and Office Depot, Jaime and Kelly were camped out at Toys R Us with a Best Buy and a Sears within their sights. We strategically placed ourselves throughout the Chicago south suburbs so that we could effectively cover all the major stores at exactly the same time. Claudia was the "lead." I was just an embedded reporter going along for the ride.

The plan was to enter the store and immediately go in opposite directions to get the "Door Busters" first. Door Busters are what I call the "lottery" items. A store will advertise a 37" HD LCD TV at a Door Buster ridiculously low price of $159 ($799 value). People begin lining up immediately following Halloween and the procession wraps around the building out to the expressway, merely to find out that there is a guarantee of only three per store. They wonder why they need cleanup in housewares, along with an ice pack and a butterfly Band-Aid.

After the first sweep, we met back at the checkout, where a cashier waited with her raised scanner in one hand and a large plastic shopping bag in the other. She was gearing up for a steady stream of shoppers and we were her inaugural sale of the day. In other words, she was still smiling.

I bought two $50 rolling jumbo-sized duffle bags (not on my list, but couldn't pass up the deal). They were priced at a rock-bottom door-busting bargain of $9.99 each. I also bought a heated mattress pad (also not on my list, but what the heck). It was 75 percent off (not counting the coupon that Claudia gave me for an additional 30 percent off my entire purchase, which would put that one into the negative column). In addition, I picked up twelve peppermint-scented candles in a jar (also not on my list) for a buck a piece! ANNNNND, the retail price of her "Showcase" is (pregnant pause) $271.36, and she only paid $23.98 for fifteen items that were not on the list. Amazing!! I was addicted!

We checked out and headed back to base camp (the car), where we had extra store flyers with coupons, a cooler of individual water bottles, hooded sweatshirts, fanny packs, a GPS, and a bag of high-protein snacks.

"Are we going to meet up with the other girls now?" I asked.

"No," Claudia said, "we always go through and buy our Door Busters first, then check out and bring them to the car so we can go back for the Early Bird Specials. Otherwise, it's too much to carry, and the lines get really long."

Made sense. I followed her lead and put my bags in the trunk. Then we both went back inside to see if we "Early Birds" could find any "worms."

There is a big difference between a Door Buster and an Early Bird. Stores will generally have an ample supply of Early Bird Special merchandise; however, it is for a limited time only. If the advertisement says Early Bird Special until 10 a.m., that's it. Just like Cinderella, if you show up at one minute past, you are walking home empty-handed, and that blouse you thought you were going to get for $14.95 suddenly has appreciated in value like oceanfront property and now is a whopping fifty-nine bucks.

I found a gorgeous men's size XL cashmere sweater that was made in the Alashan Plateau in China for ONLY $19 (normally $69). I decided to buy it and put it in the De-Graaf Family Grab Bag, where it could anonymously find its way into the hands of an ungrateful recipient. I hoped that Uncle Earl from Atlanta didn't get it. I don't think the locals in the land of cotton take kindly to Yankee transfers from Chicago who wear imported cashmere. At least I saved $50 bucks and it would appear that I went way over our usual $15 limit per gift. I would reserve the right to take credit for my contribution until I could analyze the payoff in doing so.

"Are you ready to check out?" the voice of my mother-in-law came over my radio.

"I'll meet you up there. I'm in the men's department. Do you think Uncle Earl would look good in chartreuse?" I asked.

"What are you buying for Uncle Earl?"

"It's a long story."

The line at the checkout was now twenty-five shoppers deep and double-backed through the shoe department, luggage, and coats. I felt good about myself as I noticed that the display of rolling jumbo-sized duffle bags that was full just fifteen minutes earlier was now a cold desolate shelving unit with a lonely scrap of tissue paper along with the sign that said "Door Buster Special ONLY $9.99."

It was time to "field dress" our cart. We rearranged everything so that it wasn't spilling over the front end and positioned ourselves in line behind a trio of giggling and jovial senior women with light-up reindeer antlers straddling their silver locks.

"Hey," I said, "where is the rest of your team? Did the fog machine in Electronics throw Rudolph off course again?"

"This is how we keep an eye on each other as we shop. You should try it. It's a lot of fun and it's HANDS FREE!" the woman of experience said as she shook her head slightly to make her spring-loaded antlers dance. I was quite sure these ladies also belonged to one of those red hat clubs where they dress in whatever they want, say whatever they want, and eat whatever they want. I was envious.

She also wore a fleece sweatshirt with a surplus of tiny gold bells sewn to it. I was waiting for her to start belting out "dashing through the snow, in a one horse....." She didn't. Her comrades had the same. Ingenious! Not only could this trio see each other from twenty yards, but they could also hear each other ring-a-ding-dinging with bargains in tow. I bet their perfume was strategically applied as well (gag, cough, hold my nose). A wafting trail of Jean Nate followed them throughout the store. I think that was just a coincidence.

By noon that day, I was in my driveway with a minivan filled to capacity with stuff, a wallet emptied of cash, and a credit card with a little less limit left on it. My feet were sore, but my toes had thawed with the floor heat cranked up to the max. I had to make a mad dash with my stash of gifts to the attic above the garage before the boys could see through the large plastic bags. Oh, and I had to make a few changes to my master gift list. I hoped my eighteen-year-old would like his heated mattress pad, because that deal was too sweet to pass up!

Lower Your Standards So You Can Meet Them

As much as I try to make the holidays special for our family, things have a tendency to run amuck more times than not. I have learned that the secret of a happy holiday is to lower my standards considerably!

I once finished my Christmas shopping by August, wrapped every gift, and hid them in the most obscure places—so obscure that I not only forgot where I hid them, but I forgot that I even bought them. We ended up having an impromptu celebration of April Fool's Day that year and my youngest got an inflatable sled and a hockey stick just in time for spring break. I'm not sure if I pity or envy the psychotherapist who gets that one.

On the other extreme, I've also been so last minute that one year I did ALL of our holiday shopping during a six-hour bargain hunting marathon on Christmas Eve. I got home well past midnight and hauled in the goods while not a creature was stirring. I put everything safely in my closet and set my alarm for three hours later. I figured I would recharge my batteries a bit and then get up and wrap everything and put it under the tree for the perfect Kodak holiday moment.

What started out as a "three-hour tour" ended up a "long winter's nap." Yep, I overslept and, of course, the boys beat me to the Christmas tree. *UGH!*™ I quickly quarantined them in a locked bedroom with my husband, who told them some cockamamie story about the year he got Garanimals and soap on a rope. In less than ten minutes, I had their gifts wrapped, tagged, and positioned neatly below our tree. I gave Ron the signal that we were ALL CLEAR, and he let them loose. Like racehorses at the Kentucky Derby, they charged the hallway. In two minutes' time, my picture perfect Christmas morning looked like a recycling center.

I don't recommend this method of Christmas gift buying at all. It was bad enough that my credit card hadn't cooled off from my shopping spree, but the Scotch Tape barely got a chance to stick. If I had my way, I'd be saying, "Yes, Virginia, there is a Santa Claus!"

Which, by the way, reminds me of the moment of truth that I had with our son Luke when he questioned me like the state's attorney at an O. J. Simpson trial: "Just answer the question YES or NO; is Santa real?"

That was a tough one. I had gone to great lengths to create the Santa illusion and wasn't sure I could just rat Santa out with a one-word answer. I bought special "Santa" wrapping paper that I hid in the most remote corner of our dusty attic, each year fighting a new layer of cobwebs to get to the stash. I carefully baked "Santa" cookies and ate half a raw carrot every Christmas Eve, leaving the other half on the plate. Rudolph was trying to slim down, I would explain on Christmas morning. All the gifts were tagged "From: Santa" and I recall the year that our boys asked us why they didn't get a gift from Mom and Dad.

"No, Santa isn't real." There, I said it.

With glossy eyes and an angry tone, Luke said, "You lied to me," and he crossed his arms and turned his back.

That was it. From that moment on, I made the whole Santa thing a mystery and answered all inquiries with the same phrase, "What do you think?" They would ask if there really was a North Pole, and I would reply, "What do you think?" They would ask how Santa got all around the world in one night and I would answer, "What do you think?" They would ask if Mrs. Claus ever wanted a divorce and I would say, "What do you think?"

I found that this too had its problems because that meant that my three littlest boys didn't have a definitive belief system about Santa. I equate it to looking at a senior citizen's smile or a swimsuit model's chest with the question, "Are they real?" There is always a shadow of doubt mixed in with a shred of hope that utopia does exist.

A neighbor called once to inform me that my son was telling the other children on the bus that there is no Santa.

"I am so sorry," I said. "I will talk to him." She apparently was still climbing in and out of her attic to get the special "Santa paper."

The kids were ten years old and our district was among the highest scoring on standardized tests in the state. It didn't surprise me that, at their age, they questioned the validity of a three-hundred-pound elderly man being carted to rooftops all over the world by flying reindeer and stuffing the junk in his trunk down a modern chimney. They were fairly intelligent children.

However, I understood that the adults wanted to "keep the dream alive," so I threatened to give only socks and underwear for Christmas if I got one more call from one more disappointed parent with a crying child in the background, saying, "You lied to me!"

When I was a kid, there were two places that my parents would hide our presents from Santa—under their bed, or in their closet. My brother, sister, and I would painstakingly unwrap all the gifts while Mom and Dad were at work and then rewrap them before they got home. On Christmas Eve, we would all get in the car and drive around town in the dark looking for Rudolph's red nose in the sky. Meanwhile, Grandpa Joe would be back at home pulling out all the gifts and putting them under the tree. Every year, we'd get back to the house and Grandpa would tell us how we "just missed him." If the adults only knew that we were "in" on the whole thing! We pretended to be surprised on Christmas. It was exhausting and I remember being relieved when my mom stopped "pretending" about the whole Santa thing herself. It's stressful for everyone to keep the "dream" alive.

Martha Stewart Never Ordered Pizza on Christmas Eve!

I will never forget my first disastrous stab at cooking a holiday meal. It was the day of Christmas Eve, and I was a young mom with two in diapers and a fan of the Martha Stewart show. That meant I had Martha Stewart expecta- tions with the resources of Ellie Mae Clampett (zero domes- tic skill and a half dozen monkeys on her back). My husband had to work that day, so he wasn't available to help. My baby, Luke, cried for fifteen hours without taking a breath!

I had planned a Martha-like menu of roast chicken with lemon sauce, salad with cranberries and almonds, mashed potatoes-gratin, and chocolate peppermint cake. After a full day of changing diapers, burping, feeding, cradling, consoling, rinse and repeat, I was a mess! Ron came home to a frazzled wife with a kid on each hip; and the house looked like it had been broken into; and the meat was raw in the middle because when I put it in the oven, it was still frozen. The family would be ringing our doorbell in twenty minutes.

I handed Ron a crying baby, and then put my face in my hands and joined the chorus. I was sobbing. My sweet husband was so endearing in that moment. Guys could take a lesson from his response. He quieted Luke (the kid was probably relieved to get out of the arms of what must've felt like a militant army cook) and then put an arm around me and told me that the food and the house didn't matter.

"It's Christmas," he said, "don't cry over the food. We'll order out. And as for the house, we'll just shove everything into plastic garbage bags and lock them in the basement until tomorrow."

Working like Vegas blackjack dealers, we cleared the surfaces of our small townhouse into trash bags, and then we covered the remains of my uncooked meal with foil and hid it in the fridge. Thankfully, the Pizza Hut in town was open for business. We ordered four large pepperoni pizzas and tuned our TV to the local cable station, which featured a burning log to create a makeshift fireplace. We taped our stockings to the screen and called it Christmas.

The funny thing is that Nate and Luke were too young to even remember that fiasco and my sister-in-law, Danette, recalls those simpler times with fondness and laughter. We made ordering Pizza Hut and the TV fireplace a DeGraaf tradition for several years after that. I guess if you really look hard, you can find value even in the not-so-perfect times. I learned that my husband wasn't overly concerned about me creating a magazine-worthy meal. I learned that the most important thing about Christmas was faith and family!

Ten Bucks Says You Can't NOT Be Sarcastic

One thing I noticed right away when I became a De-Graaf was that they communicate like third-string PG-rated stand-up comedians on steroids. They were never crude, never profane, but extremely sarcastic. From an outsider's perspective, it was funny at first, and then a bit disturbing when I observed that it didn't seem to have an end.

I have always been of the mind-set that a little sarcasm goes a long way, and there should be a stopping point. If a person cannot be genuinely funny without being overly critical of someone else, they should just watch *Letterman* or *The Tonight Show* and let bygones be bygones.

So, one holiday when I was hosting dinner, I taped a ten-dollar bill to the wall and said, "Anyone who gets through the whole meal without being sarcastic will get their name in a drawing for the cash."

"Like that's going to work," my brother-in-law, Marc, said.

"Ten bucks would cover Dad's haircut, but it wouldn't buy me a strong cup of coffee," my sister-in-law, Danette, said.

"If Dad paid ten bucks for THAT haircut, he paid $9.50 too much," my husband said.

"Hey, I cut Dad's hair," my mother-in-law, Claudia, said.

Obviously the DeGraafs were off and running and my little "game" was having a reverse effect. I told everyone to get their cheap shots in now because I was going to start the contest in five minutes and after that, no sarcasm allowed.

The room got deathly quiet and then Danette burst out a snicker. She controlled herself for twenty seconds more, and said, "This is stupid. Keep your ten bucks."

Sensing my desperation for a sarcasm-free holiday, Claudia sincerely complimented me on my outfit and said the pizza looked delicious! Then she challenged my father-in-law, Ron Sr., that she would win the money. That was all she needed to do. Game on!

The one thing that trumps sarcasm in the DeGraaf clan is competition. My father-in-law stood up and with a big smile said how wonderful our family is and how he cannot even count all the blessings in his life.

I could see Marc struggling to maintain composure, and then out it came. "That's because people with an IQ of sixty-five aren't expected to be able to count, Dad," he said.

"I'll give you **IQ**," Ron Sr. snapped back. "**I QUIT**."

They were both out.

It was down to me, Claudia, and my husband. My mother-in-law wouldn't take the money so that meant the money was staying in my pocket anyway, so I said, "Okay, forget it, let's go back to our old ways," and I grabbed the ten bucks and put it back in my purse.

We ate our pizza and warmed ourselves by the TV fire log and it was a very Merry DeGraaf Family Christmas!

A Mocking Bird Almost GETS it with a Tennis Racket

I used to laugh at houses that still had Christmas decorations up on Valentine's Day. That was until I became a mother of five children and realized just how exhausting one twenty-four hour period can be. Even though a task may require only ten minutes to tackle, it takes a considerable amount of stimulus to care enough to give a rip about the pinecone wreath that still hangs on the front door!

That's what happened to me one year. My Christmas wreath was still gracing the threshold of my home well into February. At least it had a red bow, I rationalized.

I finally decided to take it down when one evening, I opened the door and two birds fluttered up in my face. Apparently, one was a smart bird (that one flew out to the great outdoors), but the other was stupid. It flew into my house, which was already occupied by seven humans. That bird was going nuts dive-bombing our kitchen island and then back up to the ceiling fan—back and forth, back and forth.

Of course, you can imagine the chaos the bird had created in a houseful of young boys. The kids were all screaming and yelling for the bird to fly outside.

"Don't hurt the bird," my oldest, Nate, said.

"Will it live?" "Can we keep it?" "I want to keep it in my room," the rest of the boys blurted out.

I was silently praying it wouldn't drop a splat on my new rug or my old head. I put on a baseball cap and opened the front and the back doors, along with several windows.

It was the middle of winter in the Midwest and we are on a couple acres with wide-open fields all around us. Gale-force winds are the norm in our neighborhood, so when we opened up the house trying to convince our little visitor to go home, we invited old man winter to come right in and get comfy.

"Mom, get a sheet and tape it to the wall to block off the rest of the house and make him go out," one son suggested.

I did. It didn't help.

"Ok, get some bread and make a trail leading him outside. It will be just like Hansel and Gretel," my four-year-old, Adam said. They were reading nursery rhymes in school.

I did. It didn't help.

For forty-five minutes our family scampered to and fro chasing the bird, with open windows and doors and a loaf of Wonder bread scattered on the floor. Suddenly I felt a momentum shift in the conflict. At first, Nate was so concerned about the safety of the bird and whether or not the bird was scared.

He kept saying, "Don't hurt it. Don't scare it. Awe, it's so cute."

However, it's true what they say about the spirit being willing but the flesh is weak, because in less than an hour's time with our whole family breathing heavily and with freezing sweat dripping from our heads, my son turned into a vicious hunter. He went out to the garage and returned with a tennis racket cocked over his right shoulder.

"I don't care anymore. Just get it. Kill it. Smash it. Do whatever it takes," Nate chanted.

"Calm down, McEnroe," I said. "Let's try a new approach."

We turned off all the lights and had everyone get very quiet. The bird flew back from whence he came. Finally! We closed up the house and cranked up the heat, and I vowed to forevermore put the Christmas wreath away on New Year's Day.

12 steps to a Having a Merry Christmas and Taking the UGH!™ Out of Humbug

1. Lower your standards for yourself.

2. Lower your expectations of others.

3. Lower your credit limit.

4. Lower your commitments.

5. Lower your stress.

6. Lower your activities.

7. Lower your voice.

8. Lower your view. (see things from a childlike perspective)

9. Lower your nose. (Humility)

10. Lower your number of gifts.

11. Lower your caloric intake.

12. Lower all of the above and raise your spirits!

Chapter Four

Mustard's Last Stand

CSI Investigation

"I don't have anything nice to wear," my husband whined as he was getting ready to hop in the shower before going to the dentist. He was scheduled for a six-month cleaning. He finally realized that going to the dentist every six months beats going once every four years. He learned the hard way that procrastination is okay for clipping toenails but not so great when it comes to teeth cleaning! There is a big difference between a hole in your sock and a hole in your tooth, but that is another story.

The boys were home from school for Veterans Day and it rained—my worst nightmare. Being cooped up in a houseful of boys on a weekday when they normally would be in school made me feel like a five-year-old who just found out that Christmas was canceled!

Four teenage boys were in my basement all day playing video games, ascending occasionally to scan our kitchen cabinets, fridge, and pantry. They ate like locusts. Our nine-year-old, Adam, had three of his friends from his football team over, and they played a scrimmage game in my kitchen/living room/hallway until I made them go outside and play in the forty-degree drizzle. They lasted just long enough for them to get full of mud, track it back into the house, and demand hot chocolate.

A third friend stopped by and decided the chaos was too much for even him. Smart kid! He and my middle son, Joel, went to his house, where the only annoying sound they might encounter would be an occasional bark from one of his two dogs or his older sister saying, "I'm telling Mom you said that!"

I knew that I had reached the height of maternal desperation when I pressed my lips up to the crack of the locked bathroom door and shouted, "I'm going with you to the dentist!" It just didn't seem fair that my husband got to work all day at a job, surrounded by adults, doing meaningful and necessary work that had a beginning and an end with a promise of a paycheck at the end of the week, and then GET TO go to the dentist, while I was trapped struggling to work from home while simultaneously coordinating a defensive line and a "feed the children" program.

I have a very hard time concentrating with ten boys rummaging through my kitchen and running up and down the stairs. At least I could read a lady's magazine in the waiting area of the dental office for thirty minutes. Pathetic! I started to look for a decent shirt for Ron to put on while he flossed his teeth for the first time in six months.

I went through his shirt-stuffed closet (an unimpressive three-foot long hanging bar) to find something for him. I kept finding shirts that were either too small, had stains, or that he no longer wore. Most often if an item met one of the first two criteria, it automatically fell into the "no longer wear" category. The one exception is the perfectly good, never worn, pink polo shirt that I bought for him two years ago (I think it was a Black Friday Door Buster). I told him that "all the guys are wearing pink these days." I think he refused to wear it just to spite me. He also refused to acknowledge the money I saved when I came home and said, "Look at this awesome pink shirt I bought for you, hon! I saved $37.50!"

"No, you SPENT $12.50 on a pink shirt," he said. He never even tried it on. I would have been better off spending the $12.50 on postage stamps and entering the sweepstakes at Publishers Clearing House. At least there was a minuscule chance of a return on my investment.

In my search for a respectable shirt for Ron to wear to the dentist, I noticed something. I am quite confident other wives encounter this dilemma as well. I laid out four or five nice shirts on the bed. Each one had a big food stain in exactly the same location—the left center, lower chest section of the front. Yes, he is right-handed and apparently has a hole in the left side of his face. What surprised me was the distance that the food had to travel in order to land in the stained location. These weren't just tiny beads of egg drop soup stains. These were man-sized stains that were surely made from large heavy chunks of beef or chicken or sausage.

His stained collection of shirts reminded me of my maternity tops from years gone by. I would always get a food stain in the area where my belly was the widest. (Now, the widest part of me follows me wherever I go, and I can only hope there are no stains back there!) Could it be that my husband's waistline had expanded and the stain was indicative of the widest part of his midsection? It was a theory.

I considered starting a private investigative company: CSI (Clothing Stain Investigation). But I thought better of it since guys don't really care, and it's not going to change their behavior one bit; so why bother figuring out how it happened if you can't control why it happens?

I should tell my husband that I think a full beard is wildly sexy in hopes that a fluffy poof of hair on his chin may catch at least a small percentage of the mess. It's doubtful. Perhaps a gigantic "bib vest" like the construction workers who work along the roadside wear. That might be the answer. If it could be made manly enough, guys could strap on the bib vest before meals and let it take the brunt of their food stain abuse, thus sparing their shirts.

After the dentist visit, I convinced Ron to take me out for a bite to eat. I had to justify the fact that I went with him; plus, I wasn't quite ready to go back home (the kids would still be awake). We went to Applebee's and ordered a combo appetizer platter of BBQ Boneless Chicken, cheese sticks, and artichoke dip. Our waitress accidentally bumped my husband's water glass while refilling it at the exact moment that he was about to enjoy a big hunk of BBQ chicken. It flopped off the tip of his fork and landed smack-dab on the left center lower chest of the front of his shirt! *UGH!*™ There goes another one.

Eggs Do NOT Belong In My Sink

"What are you up to down there?" I called to Adam (who was about three at the time). I was upstairs in my bedroom, getting ready for yet another relaxing Saturday of doing a half dozen loads of laundry, mixed with toilet scrubbing between spin cycles.

"Nothin'."

I knew better. It was way too quiet and all mothers of toddler boys know that quiet means one of two things—the kid has either downright exhausted himself, and he is now sleeping upright in some corner of the house wearing only his underwear and a football helmet; OR, he is up to no good.

Well, in this case, "Nothin'" definitely meant SOME-THIN'! I entered the kitchen to find that my darling Adam had taken all of the eggs out of the refrigerator and cracked them in the sink. He had dumped a full gallon of milk in the sink and was in the process of folding in a five-pound package of flour.

"WHAT are you doing?" I beseeched an answer even though I knew that whatever the answer was, it would make absolutely NO sense to me and perfect sense to him. *UGH!*™

"I'm making pancakes in the sink. These are the ones that I didn't get any shells in," he said with pride, pointing to four messy eggshells on the counter.

My entire kitchen looked like a giant Bismarck filled with raw egg. Yum!

"What on earth possessed you to make this mess?" I asked, again knowing that whatever he answered could not justify his actions.

"I wanted to make pancakes just for you, Mommy!" he returned with an adorable dimple-faced smile.

A mother's quandary—how to handle this one, I thought to myself. His intentions were noble; he wanted to make pancakes for me. How precious! I would never turn pancakes down if my husband offered to treat me with such admiration and regality, and he would make a giant mess and expect me to clean it up too. So, I couldn't really discipline him from the standpoint of having done something evil. However, he needed to know that making a huge mess and wasting all of our groceries wouldn't cut it.

I took Adam aside for a twenty-five minute lecture and reminded him of our commitment to fighting world hunger by ensuring that the voracious eaters in our own household would be able to carry on. I told him that creating messes unnecessarily could lead to our family being investigated for squalor, and that even children his age and with his dimples could be carted off by well-meaning government employees who would promptly place him in a home with perfect strangers who vacuumed daily!

Okay, I didn't really tell him that, but I wanted to. I basically just tried to reason with him, which was a complete waste of carbon dioxide. And then, I sent him to his room to give ME a time-out! I needed a chance to collect myself and make an attempt to get the flour dust off of the rooster light hanging over my kitchen island. That rooster needed a bath anyway.

My budding "Food Network" star came bouncing back into the kitchen about twenty minutes later. Along with cleaning the rooster light, I had taken out the trash, cleaned the counters, put the dishes in the dishwasher, and made the kitchen look like nothing ever happened. I was sitting at the kitchen table enjoying a freshly brewed cup of coffee and putting "eggs" on my grocery list. I took the opportunity to reinforce our earlier conversation and make sure that Adam had learned his lesson.

"Now, son, you're not going to do THAT again, are you?" to which Adam instantly replied without hesitation and with a shrug of his shoulders, "Nope! There are no more eggs!" *UGH!*™

Is It a Sin to Wear Dirty Underwear to Church?

Getting our entire family to church on Sunday morning is a miracle nothing short of Moses and his Red Sea crossing. Let's just say that it can be an out-of-body experience like no other!

I used to have a much higher standard for our prechurch prep, but over the years, my expectations have been on a steady decline. When we had our first two sons, our typical American family of four looked the "churchy" part—boys in center-creased dress pants with buttoned-up collared shirts and hair combed neatly to the left.

Today, my only request for our tribe of five is that they are dressed and that their clothes have no holes and no dirt. At least I draw the line at allowing my boys to wear dirt to church!

I will never forget one Sunday morning when the Devil definitely was trying to keep us home! We got up late and as my husband was about to step into the shower, he asked me if I would find him a pair of clean underwear. "Sure thing," I said and assured him that there was a load of clean underwear and socks in the dryer.

Wrong!

No socks and underwear in the dryer (only towels). No clean undies on top of the dryer or in the pile of clean clothes that were half stacked and half scattered on the couch. (I really need to stop folding laundry while watching TV. It's pointless! The stuff gets knocked down, folded again, and yes, even knocked down once more.)

I was running out of options as Ron was running out of hot water. Now what? I did what any quick-thinking and resourceful woman would do; I shuffled through the dirty clothes and found the "cleanest" pair of dirty underwear that I could. I shook them and neatly folded them in exactly the same way I have been folding Ron's boxer/briefs for almost two decades (which, by the way, I find pointless). They looked a little stretched out, so I pressed extra hard to try and smooth over a few of the wrinkles and placed them on the closed lid of the toilet seat next to the shower.

"Here you go, babe," I said without another word.

I continued scrambling to get the rest of the gang in our minivan. It was complete chaos (normal for us). Three of the boys were fighting, one couldn't find his other shoe, and one was still sleeping. Somehow, we managed to all get in the van for the fifteen-minute trip to church. (I swear I could walk on fire!) *UGH!*™

Ron was quiet for the whole ride with a stern look on his face, and his lips all bunched up in a knot. As we pulled into the church parking lot, I turned to him and said, "What's wrong?"

"THESE underwear aren't clean, are they?" he said. He was so ticked. The droop in his backside was probably a dead giveaway. I actually had all but forgotten about the dirty underwear that I tried to pass off as freshly washed. I jumped over a thousand hurdles just to get seven breathing bodies to church ONLY five minutes late that morning, and it slipped my mind that my husband was actually wearing day-old underwear.

"NO THEY ARE NOT!" I jolted back and pulled my shirt up to my neck and said, "What are you complaining about, I am wearing MY SWIMSUIT!" (I really couldn't find ANY clean underwear!) I had no earthly idea what the boys were wearing, and I wasn't about to ask.

I was pretty sure that God was more concerned about the condition of our hearts and not so worried about the fact that Ron was worshipping in his dirty undies and that I had my swimsuit on! After all, God has a sense of humor!!

Lots of Boys Make Indoor Thunderstorms

If only I could find a way to capture the vim and vigor within a boy, refine it, and send it to market. Warren Buffet and I would be Facebook friends! Okay, maybe not; but it is a good idea, and if I could pull it off, I'd be a household name and the United States wouldn't be so dependent on foreign energy.

When my husband built our home, he put extra insulation between all of the walls. Our carpenter thought it was pointless since you really couldn't affect the R value of insulation by putting it in interior walls.

"This has nothing to do with saving energy," we told the carpenter. "We are hoping to eliminate some of the boy-noise."

This is one of many decisions I have grown to regret—along with the selection of cream-colored carpet we *HAD* before two of our sons opened up a giant-sized bottle of chocolate syrup, turned it upside down, and vigorously squeezed it while running circles around our living room playing "birthday party." That was over fifteen years ago and when we had to pick a new color, I told the salesman at the flooring store that I wanted the color of "dirt" please!

By the way, that syrup fiasco was actually covered by our home owner's policy. My cousin Karen worked for an insurance agency at the time, and when I told her what my brilliant children had done, she told me to call my insurance company to see if they would cover it. To my surprise, they did. They called it a "natural disaster." From that day, I have NEVER purchased another giant-sized bottle of chocolate syrup.

I regretted the interior insulation decision too because it didn't really do much to cut down on the boy-noise; but it did, however, make it impossible for my boys to hear me when I called them from downstairs. We should have known that King Kong could not be contained by mere humans!

That King Kong–type of energy in a boy seems to rev up right before bedtime. It's almost like their bodies sense that they are about to enter into eight to twelve hours of inactivity, so they want to exert a fury of liveliness before such constriction. Once, while plopped in the corner of our leather sectional with my feet comfortably crossed on the matching ottoman and enjoying intermittent consciousness, I was suddenly awakened to what I thought was a thunderstorm.

Rumble, rumble, rumble, rummmmmmmmmmble. Slam.

"What the heck was that?" I asked my husband, who was occupied with *Wheel of Fortune*.

Silence.

Rumble, rumble, rumble, rummmmmmmmmmble. Slam.

"There it is again," I insisted!

Silence followed by giggling.

"L" shrieked my husband! "You need an L," he yelled louder and with both arms waving. He didn't hear the "thunder," nor did he feel the slight vibration of our entire house.

The boys had created a "game" where they took turns running a gauntlet. They tightly rolled tube socks into large "bullets" (I finally figured out how the socks got all wadded up like that in the wash) and whipped them at each other as they raced from one end of the hallway to the other. Every pillow in the house was stacked into bunkers, and I was reminded of our failed attempt to soundproof the boy-noise!

"KNOCK IT OFF RIGHT NOW!" I roared.

Rumble, rumble, rumble, rummmmmmmmmmble. Slam.

"It's ALL IN THE FAMILY HEIRLOOM," Ron yelled again at the TV. "How STUPID can you be? L, L, L!!!"

Rumble, rumble, rumble, rummmmmmmmmmmble. Crash! I heard one of the framed pictures hanging in our upstairs hallway finally give up its hold and fall to the floor. Well, I thought, there went another "family heirloom!"

Who Licked My Hot Dog Bun?

"Mom! Where did my hot dog go?" my youngest son Caleb asked.

"I don't know. It was right there," I said as I pulled yet another empty orange juice carton from the refrigerator to make room for the leftover chili.

"I put a hot dog on your plate two seconds ago. What happened to it?" I asked.

"Somebody took it," Caleb said. The guilty party (Adam) was in the living room deeply engulfed in the second half of a football game on TV. He confessed, saying, "I didn't see your name on it!" That didn't comfort Caleb at all. He took it personally like someone just stole his teddy bear.

"Hey," I said, "around here, you need to keep your hands on your food until it reaches your mouth or you'll be wearing jeans with an elasticized waist until you're twenty-five."

"Yeah, take it from Mom," a voice came from behind the sectional, "she knows how to keep some meat on her bones." A wry comment from one of my teenagers.

I fixed another hot dog for Caleb and then continued running around collecting dirty dishes from under the couch, next to the computer, on the end table, the coffee table, and the back of the toilet tank.

Caleb went into my office (our old dining room) and got out a Sharpie permanent marker. I observed him walk back to his plate with determination as if on a mission. I thought he was actually going to write his name on his hot dog.

"Stop! You can't write with permanent marker on a hot dog and then eat it!" I warned. To which my seven-year-old said, "Don't be silly, Mom. I'm writing my name on my pop can. I licked my hot dog bun so no one would take it!"

"Did you lick the first hot dog too?" asked the red-hot thief (aka Adam) in front of the TV.

"Yeah, and you got my cooties," Caleb said.

"You did not, you big fat liar," Adam said.

I can't wait to see my boys at their weddings. They'll all be sitting in tuxedos at the head table with one arm forming a circular barrier around their plates while licking the dinner rolls with the other!

The 10 Commandments
to Survive the Weekly Food Bill

Food has become a commodity around our house. It's used as leverage, bartered, battled over, hidden, rationed, labeled, and now apparently licked! I'm guilty of hoarding as well. I keep my Diet Coke and M&Ms either hidden in my bra drawer, my jumbo box of Super Tampons (then I know they are there when I NEED them), or safely locked in the trunk of my car. All are excellent hiding places!

I've made many attempts to maintain order in the culinary department, but most have ended in complete failure. So, I decided to just put forward a few general commandments and hope that I covered my bases.

Commandment #1
Thou Shall NOT Have False Food Fights!

Food fights in our house are not the kind you see in the typical preteen Disney Channel movie, where kids whip mashed potatoes at each other. My children would never let a helping of mashed potatoes go to waste.

When my boys have a food fight, they literally fight over the food! They had the mother of all food fights over a brown sugar Pop Tart one day that practically sent me to the moon! General Patton would have been impressed with their tenacious spirit for battle, but I was just plain livid! I put my right hand over my chest, raised my left, and proclaimed: "It will be a cold day in Phoenix the next time I buy a box of brown sugar Pop Tarts."

It's just a matter of supply and demand. People who live in big families with five growing boys who can eat two portions of lasagna, three pieces of garlic bread (skip the fresh green salad), and still have room for dessert are going to have to get smart about it. You can only split a Twinkie into so many pieces.

My teenagers have their own jobs, a driver's license, and access to my vehicle; so they occasionally will buy "forbidden foods" and hide them around the house. Once they took out the bag inside the "sticks and twigs healthy cereal," and hid their Cocoa Puffs inside. I caught them red-handed when they were getting a late-night snack. I thought they were constipated and looking for more fiber. I've since discovered that there is no such thing as a constipated teenager. They eat so much junk food that their plumbing is in constant flow.

Commandment #2
Thou Shall NOT Have a Five-Second Rule!

The "five-second" rule doesn't exist at our house. If something falls to the floor and isn't visibly covered in dust or hair, it's edible. It's considered a genetic test of our immune system. Just pick it up and eat it. "Pretend you're camping!" I always say.

Commandment #3
Thou Shall Consume Thy Food by the Expiration Day Plus a Day or Two

Expiration dates, I tell my family, are suggestions. The dairy people just don't want to get sued if you eat their stuff and throw up or get gout. And, my family doesn't know this, but when my little guys leave for school in the morning with half full glasses of milk on the table, that is when I pour them back into the milk jug and designate that one for KIDS ONLY. We buy half a dozen gallons of milk per week, so I will just open up a new jug for "adults only" and let the boys drink out of the other one. They don't know the difference. Hey, milk is expensive!

Commandment #4
Thou Shall Not Be Afraid of a Little Mold

"Mold is medicine!" I told my husband during an evening meal early on in our marriage. I made tacos and the cheese had spent a little too much time in the fridge. I spotted green on the bright orange shredded cheddar only after he had already eaten one taco. So, I figured it was too late, and I might as well try not to alarm him. Instead, I tried to distract him and brisk off the fuzzy green substance on the remaining tacos without him noticing, but he caught me. That was just the first of many "mealtime experiences" that my dear husband would encounter. He has a pretty strong stomach!

Commandment #5
Thou Shall Not Leave an Empty Container
in the Fridge or Pantry

I absolutely do not understand why my guys do that. They will drink all but one tablespoon of a carton of orange juice and put it back in the fridge. They will leave the empty Popsicle box in the freezer. They will munch through the bag of potato chips and leave it in the pantry with just crumbs in the bottom. Why? Why? Why? And it really frosts my cookies when I find a full gallon of milk left out on the kitchen table overnight after a late-night cereal binge.

Commandment #6
Thou Shall Not Complain About
Not Having Anything Good to Eat

"Do you want a nice hot bowl of oatmeal?" I asked my twelve-year-old son on a brisk Monday morning while he was getting ready for school.

"No."

"Do you want a bagel?" I asked.

"No."

"How about a bowl of cereal?"

"Naaaa."

"Pancakes?"

"No, we NEVER have ANYTHING good to eat."

"There are restaurants with fewer choices on their menus!" I said. "What is wrong with having something decent for breakfast?"

He liked me much better when I used to buy PopTarts and Cocoa Puffs. Well, those days are gone, because not only did the War of the Brown Sugar Pop Tart do me in, but I made a "sugar-free" commitment to Caleb's teacher because that kid was already halfway to LaLa Land without sugar. If I gave him sugar cereal for breakfast, I would be getting a call from the school for sure!

"Have a banana, and get out to the bus!" I said.

Commandment #7
Thou Shall Eat What Is in
Front of Thy Face and Not Complain

"It's macaroni and cheese!" I said. "Can't you tell? It's homemade!"

Neither my husband nor any of my children ate my one attempt at homemade macaroni and cheese! I was so disappointed. It took a lot more time and effort than just ripping open a box, saving the top for the PTO, and boiling water.

"Forget this," I said, and I never made it again. It's so discouraging to plan a meal, shop for ingredients, prepare everything only to have your family say, "I like the box kind better." It's equally as annoying to cook a large meal and find out when the timer goes off that your husband had a late lunch and two of the kids are skipping dinner to go to basketball practice, while a third is sound asleep on the couch. That leaves me and two children to eat a twelve-pound turkey!

Commandment #8
Thou Shall Not Graze All Day Long

When the boys are not at school and are home all day, they eat like cattle. They graze all day long. The kitchen never closes. It's madness. It's especially annoying if they can't be outside because of bad weather. With five of them in the house, we should install a revolving door on our refrigerator and a conveyer belt from the pantry to the kitchen table.

Commandment #9
Thou Shall Not Make Smacking
Noises with Thy Lips

The smacking of one's lips should coincide with the smacking of one's face! This is a tough one for me. When I was growing up, my family lived in a very old house with an extremely tiny kitchen. My dad installed a Formica countertop against the wall that we pulled bar stools up to, and that was where we ate. My sister, Kelli, and I sat next to each other, followed by our brother, Shane, with Mom at one end and Dad at the other. My dad must've had short lunch breaks at work because he inhaled his evening meal faster than you could say, "Please pass the bread crumb buttered noodles."

Dad also had a tendency to smack his lips while he ate and it drove Kelli and me crazy. I would bear it; but poor Kelli just couldn't do it. She would get up and leave. Now that I have my own family and lip smacking still drives me crazy, I don't let my boys do that while they eat. My boys swear that I am the ONLY ONE who cares about lip smacking. I beg to differ! The really tough part comes in when their friends are eating at our house, and they are lip smackers. Then, I do what Kelli did, and I get up and leave.

Commandment #10
Thou Shall Say, Thanks Mom, You're the Best!

A little appreciation goes a very long way with mothers. My little Caleb will come up to me and hug and kiss me and say, "Thanks, Mom, you're the best!" for a simple thing like allowing him to watch a TV show or play a video game or eat a granola bar. I love that! Sometimes all a mom needs is to know that she is appreciated and loved!

Chapter Five

IT Happens

The First of Many Notable Events

Who isn't fascinated with the diversity and function of the human anatomy from time to time? My boys seem to be especially fixated on what kind of noises and smells they can manufacture. They have a way of turning an everyday bodily function into an "event," and they seem to take pride in their own nastiness.

I remember the time I was going to show off Nate, my firstborn, to my coworkers. He was only a few weeks old. I was on maternity leave and decided to take him into the office for a premiere of sorts. I worked at the local junior college and wanted to wheel him in his stroller from department to department, stopping work as everyone ooooed and ahhhhed over my new baby.

I gave him a bath and dressed him in a virgin white sailor suit, complete with a captain's hat. He looked like a miniversion of a redheaded Richard Gere from *An Officer and a Gentleman,* and he smelled like Baby Magic. Nate was perfect in every way and ready for his Mufasa/Simba moment of presentation.

I pulled into the parking lot and got his stroller out of my trunk. It was a hot day in July and I was sweating like a pig as I snapped open the stroller and loaded it with my purse and an eighteen-pound diaper bag. (By the time I had my fifth baby, I only carried a single diaper with a travel pack of wipes; but I was new at mothering, so I had extra bottles, binkies, bibs, blankets, and clothes for a week.)

When I lifted my son out of his car seat, I could smell that something was amiss. Further inspection of his backside confirmed that indeed the "poop deck" needed swabbing! In those days, disposable diapers didn't have leakguards, no Velcro closures, and no fancy elastic. They were diapers. Period.

He had yellowish mustard-looking newborn baby poop from his shoulders to his ankles. I didn't know little babies could produce such quantities of "IT," but he did. So much for showing him off! What I needed to do was hose him off. I did the best I could and cleaned him up right there in the stroller with wipes. I changed his diaper and put a pair of old footie pjs on him that my mother-in-law's mom got at a garage sale. Good thing I had that eighteen-pound diaper bag with all the extras inside. He was clean and comfortable and just as cute as ever.

I took him inside and introduced him to all of my friends. Everyone congratulated me and that was the beginning of a long history of notable "events." My friend Terri held Nate close and kissed his head. "Babies always smell so good!" she said. She wouldn't have said that if she smelled him fifteen minutes earlier. *UGH!*™ The joys of motherhood and unexpected surprises!

Burger King Play Place and the Poopy Pants Biter

When I was growing up in a small town in Midwestern America, we didn't have a fast-food restaurant. We had a diner and a confectionary (I worked at both during high school) but no "fast food." However, there was a bigger town about fifteen minutes away that had a shopping district. There was a Sandy's Hamburger joint there. It was awesome. We didn't get to go much, but I remember our few trips and eating burgers that came in wrappers and fries that came in paper cartons. Eventually, McDonald's and Burger King made their way into the heartland, and McDonald's debuted the outdoor play place. It had a statue of the Hamburgler and a Mayor McCheese that kids could climb into. Sandy's eventually closed.

Today, most Burger Kings and McDonald's have a play area that is enclosed within the restaurant. Wow! Kids today really have it made. They have tubes and slides and big areas filled with plastic balls for them to enjoy.

When I was a young mom, I took my boys to the local Burger King on a regular basis. I would meet several other mom-friends there with their kids, and we would sit around talking while our children played.

Once we went there when it was very crowded. Kids were all over the place. In fact, the tables in the play area were all taken, so my friends and I had to sit on the outside of the glass wall that separated the play area from the rest of the restaurant. Honestly, we didn't mind at all. We could still see the children; we just didn't have to hear them.

I was busy enjoying rare conversation with adults when I heard a bloodcurdling scream that raised the hair on my neck. A little girl at the bottom of the slide had let out the howl. I went inside to find out what was the matter, and the little girl's dad had come to her aid.

"What happened?" I asked.

"That little redheaded boy BIT her," he said.

That little redheaded boy was MY three-year-old, Nate.

"I will see if I can find his mother," I told the dad and walked away. The dad gathered up his daughter and her arm with an impression of my son's upper set of teeth on it, and they left.

I went back into the play area and Nate KNEW he was in deep do-do. He was perched at the top of the slide like a bird on a wire, and wasn't moving.

"You come down here right now, young man!" I said.

"No," Nate said.

"Don't make me come up there, young man!" I said, knowing that there was no way that I could get my tush up that slide even if I wanted to, but he didn't know that.

Nate glared at me with great concentration and without uttering a word. He looked almost as if he was holding his breath. Then I could smell it! Oh yes, he DID IT. He pooped his pants. Yes, he was potty-trained but the number two skill is always the last one mastered for boys. They are usually just too busy to stop and sit for a minute. Maybe that is why boys stand to pee. I've always wondered.

Well, to my great dismay, I had to wriggle my way through a net maze to get to the top of the slide and once I finally got up there, he slid down. I wriggled back. Finally, I got my hands on Nate, and BOY WAS I MAD! I let him sit in his IT all the way home (which was more punishment for me than it was for him). When we got home, I cleaned him up, had a stern conversation with him, put him in bed, and banned play places for a month! That will show him! Ha!

He never bit anyone again, and I was never quite sure why he did it in the first place and whether or not it had anything to do with him and his "movement." Some things are better left unsaid. No, I don't regret denying that I was his mother. I knew that I would eventually have to claim him; I just didn't want to do it at that moment—nothing wrong with that, in my book.

A Clogged Toilet Puts Extra Chocolate on the Donuts

It was spring break, and I was babysitting my niece and nephew for the week. My sister, Kelli, didn't have anyone to look after the children during the week they were off of school, so they came to my house. I was working, but only part-time, and I had the week off. I lived over a hundred miles from Kel so didn't get to see them as often as I would have liked. Having the kids at my house for spring break would work out wonderfully because my niece Shana (who was eleven years old) loved babies and at the time, my youngest, Caleb, was under a year old. My next son, Adam, was three, Joel was five, Luke was ten, and Nate was eleven.

My nephew Ben would love it too because he was nine at the time, and he fit in nicely with my two oldest boys.

So, there I was with seven children under the age of eleven. Mary Poppins I was not. I had no carpetbag of tricks and no east wind with a magic umbrella that would save me or the children if things got a little crazy.

I wanted to capitalize on having Shana with me for the week and since she did such a great job at entertaining the little ones, I decided to paint my living room. I was sick of looking at white walls, so I bought paint and started taping off the trim and the ceiling. What in the world was I thinking?

I chose for the walls a deep dark red color called "Scarlet Letter." It took a coat of primer plus two coats of paint for proper coverage. By the end of the day, my thighs were screaming from all that up and down on the ladder. The kids kept interrupting me to referee squabbles, find a remote, and feed seven growling tummies at regular intervals. By the end of the week, I was physically, mentally, and emotionally bankrupt! Early on that last morning was when IT hit the fan.

I was on the ladder once again touching up the spots where I hit the white ceiling with "Scarlet Letter" by mistake. With a tiny paintbrush in hand, I strained my neck to get into the tight corners of my small living room. I had made an early morning run to Dunkin' Donuts so the kids would have more than enough sugar to get them revved up for their final day of "spring break," which was certainly no break at all for me.

A Dunkin' Donuts box of frosted donuts with sprinkles sat open in the middle of my kitchen table. It was raining outside. Most of the kids were either around the table or trying to crawl up my ladder, except for Ben and Luke, who were MIA.

Joel noticed water coming through the kitchen light fixture on the ceiling just above the box of donuts. He said, "Mommy, it's raining INSIDE!" For just a moment, I sort of had to put that information into a new box in my head.

It's raining inside? I thought. *Hmmmm. How strange.* Then I heard two adolescent boys call me from upstairs, "Mom, MOM, MM-MMMMOOOOOOMMMMM, hurry, come quick."

It was Ben and Luke. Someone had gone "number two" in a big way in the boys' upstairs bathroom, and those two geniuses were trying to get it to go down using the plunger, all the while flushing repeatedly. It was the repetitive flushing that got them into trouble. That bathroom was geographically positioned directly above the light fixture that hung over my kitchen table and that "indoor rain" that was falling on our open box of donuts was actually "poop soup" from the overflowing toilet upstairs. *UGH!*™

I shut off the water at the base of the toilet to stop the "bleeding." Then I grabbed several rolls of paper towels to soak up the flood on the bathroom floor. Once I got that situation under control, I ran back downstairs just in time to swipe a longjohn out of my son Nate's hand (who was unaware of the chaos happening one floor above him).

"You can't eat that, Nate," I told him. "There is a little extra chocolate on those donuts."

"But I love chocolate," he said.

"Trust me, you don't want to eat that," I replied and I threw the box away. He looked confused.

I disinfected the light fixture, the lightbulbs, the ceiling, the table, the chairs, all the place mats, and even the doorknobs. I told all the children to brush their teeth and rinse with Listerine. You can never be too careful.

I decided to clean off my paintbrush and put away the ladder and give the kids my undivided attention. I helped Shana and Ben get their sleeping bags and backpacks into the car and we all piled into my van to drive them to the halfway point to meet their mom. We usually met at a small town Dairy Queen to exchange children. She was already there when I arrived with my entourage, and she was enjoying a peanut buster parfait with hot fudge (my favorite).

"Do you want one?" she asked. Normally, I wouldn't turn down chocolate, but for some reason, it looked unappetizing to me.

"No thanks," I said and told her about our adventurous day. She laughed, shook her head, and said, "I swear, you could write a book!" Hmmmm.

The Little Boy Who Proved Too Much for "Mrs. Kravitz"

Every neighborhood has a Mrs. Kravitz, the friendly, nosy neighbor from one of my favorite classic television sitcoms *Bewitched*. "Mrs. Kravitz" is the indispensable chronicler of information in the cul-de-sac. She knows when lunch money is due, what time the Christmas program starts, and exactly how much was contributed toward Teacher Appreciation Week. "Mrs. Kravitz" also knows when the gas man is coming to read the meter; she knows if UPS attempted a delivery at your house while you were at work; and she *definitely* knows if one of your kids got in trouble on the bus!

Our "Mrs. Kravitz" lived not far from me, and she also babysat for extra cash. I was working part-time and made arrangements to have my youngest son, Caleb, go to "Mrs. Kravitz's" house while I worked. It was a wonderful thing to drop him off at her neat-as-a pin home with her big smile and childlike voice that traveled several octaves higher than normal when she would say, "Okay, honey, now say bye-bye to Mommy, and you will see her later."

Hugs, kisses, and I was outta there.

Well, my boy proved to be a little too much for "Mrs. Kravitz."

"Tracy DeGraaf, you have a call on line one. Tracy De-Graaf, line one. It's urgent." The page rang throughout the intercom system at the local church where I was a part-time employee. I picked up the phone.

"Hi, this is Tracy."

Silence.

"Hello."

More silence.

I heard a whimper. "Mrs. Kravitz, is that you?"

"I don't know *WHY* he would do this!" she cried.

"Who did what?" I asked.

"Caleb ruined two dresses that my girls were going to wear in my brother's wedding next month," she said through speech that was broken with tears.

"WHAT?!?" My hand went over my mouth in disbelief. Not that I didn't believe he could do something like that, but that he actually did.

"I just don't understand *WHY* he would *DO* that," she said looking for a motive.

"Do what? What did he do?" I asked again.

"My daughters are going to be the flower girls and now these dresses are a total mess. And, it's on the bed and the carpet and *EVERYTHING.*" Her words were coming faster and faster, and her breathing seemed labored.

"How did he ruin the dresses?" I persisted.

"With lipstick!" she said. "He marked them up with red lipstick—*A LOT* of bright red lipstick," she said.

"Where in the world did Caleb get LIPSTICK?" I asked, as I was pretty sure I hadn't put any lipstick in his diaper bag. He was two years old and had never worn lipstick previously. Perhaps he was hiding something.

Then the whole story unfolded. Apparently, "Mrs. Kravitz" had instructed my little lipstick-swinging maniac to take a nap in her spare bedroom, which also housed her supply of cosmetic products. "Mrs. Kravitz" was quite the entrepreneur. In addition to babysitting, she was also a cosmetics representative.

There was a basketful of tiny lipstick samples on the end table next to the bed that my little champ was napping in. Every free lipstick that I ever got was the most obnoxious deep dark color that I had ever seen. These samples were no exception. The two dresses in question were pure white, freshly pressed, sleeveless, tea length gowns with a white satin ribbon belting each, and neatly hanging on the swing arm of a brass floor lamp next to the end table. Apparently, my curious fellow explored the basket of colors and found his canvas on the skirts of the two dresses. Disaster!!

"Mrs. Kravitz, I want you to hang up with me, and call a professional dry cleaner immediately. Tell them exactly what happened and follow their instructions implicitly. Don't try to get the stains out yourself—that will only make it worse. Don't worry about the cost; I will pay for everything. Just call them right now, okay?"

"Okay." Sniffle sniff sniff, and she blew her nose and hung up.

I put the phone down and hung my head for a moment because this was Caleb's second strike with poor "Mrs. Kravitz." A week or so earlier, I was at work and "Mrs. Kravitz" called and tearfully retold how my son had made the backseat of her minivan look like a half-eaten bowl of brownie batter. Caleb had made a complete mess with a chocolate bar that she had given him. Personally, I would never waste a perfectly good chocolate bar on anyone who wasn't at least thirty-five years old and exhibiting two or more symptoms of PMS, but that's just me!

While these incidents were unwelcome, they were not, by any stretch, a surprise to me. Caleb was a bit on the curious side. He once took a blue permanent marker and randomly drew huge circles and streaks on the white walls of my bedroom. If you stood back about five or six feet from the "artwork" and looked closely, you could see a caricature of Jay Leno. He nailed the chin for sure! He also did time in "time-out" for writing on our kitchen cabinets with the same blue marker.

Mr. Clean's Magic Eraser got the marker off and is responsible for the continuation of the young boy's life. And, today, years later, that same cabinet now has "character" of its own.

I took the doors off before they fell off as a result of our big family opening and closing them a zillion times a day. I made the mistake of putting snack foods instead of canned beets in there. My boys wore the hinges out in less than three years.

Thankfully, Mrs. Kravitz's dresses were salvaged by the dry cleaner, to the tune of eighty bucks. (This was much more than my meager salary for the day's work in God's kingdom, but such is life. My reward will be in heaven, right?!)

The final straw came a week or two later when "Rembrandt" decided to change his color palette to the browns. With no brown lipstick or permanent markers within reach, Caleb found an ample supply of "color" right inside his very own diaper. In an attempt to keep my kid away from her lipstick stash, "Mrs. Kravitz" had moved his nap place to her master bedroom.

Yes, smearing IT on your babysitter's bed (the carpeting got it too) is a deal-breaker. STRIKE THREE, YOU'RE OUT! We all agreed to make different child-care arrangements before "Mrs. Kravitz" was hauled off by ambulance to take care of that racing heart rate. I hope we don't have to move. AGAIN!

By the way, I found a preschool/day care that had a structured class where they allowed the kids to draw, paint, and color to their heart's desire (and they had supervised group naps). I also invested in lots of safe washable markers and paints for him to have at home; and with supervised "creative sessions," turns out Caleb is quite the artist. I am looking at a framed piece of his original artwork that is hanging on my office wall right now. Just goes to show you what can be accomplished when you channel energy in the right direction.

Why Are Men in the Ladies Room?

There are a few perks that come with being the only female living in a house with six males. Nobody takes my clothes, my makeup, or my Kotex. And, once the boys were potty-trained (YES, I regret teaching them to stand) and once they no longer "went" in their pants, it was my husband who had to take them to the restroom whenever we were in public. This was a benefit I rather enjoyed—until a weekend getaway at an indoor water park.

We went to the water park with our extended DeGraaf family. All the in-laws and cousins were together for a three-day weekend of indoor water fun. My littlest guy, Caleb, was five years old and he loved it. There were waterslides with varying degrees of twists and turns. There was a huge bucket that held a thousand gallons of water. It automatically dumped all the water out on the half hour with a dinging bell that made kids gather underneath for a thorough washing from the rushing rapid. And, of course, there was a lazy river and a wave pool.

My husband, Ron, was hanging out with our older boys and some of our nieces and nephews on the more adventurous attractions of the park, while Caleb and I were chillaxing in the family hot tub. All of a sudden, Caleb looked at me with the urgency of a woman about to deliver triplets in the parking lot of Wal-Mart. With wide eyes and in a loud voice, while positioning both hands behind his backside, he stood up and declared, "I HAVE TO POOOOOOP!" You should have seen the faces of the other hot tubbers. I thought we would all die!

Just a few years earlier, Caleb had cleared the baby pool of a different indoor water park for a few hours while the staff did a complete "biohazard" cleanup. Those swim diapers don't do a darned thing when push comes to shove. I denied knowing him.

Anyway, the kid looked like he was about to "GO," so we hurried and ran-walked to the restroom. We looked like sprinting penguins on the slippery pavement. I followed him in, hoping he could hold it. He quickly opened the door of the bathroom stall.

How strange, I thought, *there is only one stall in here.* I also found it peculiar that there was a father and son to my right who were standing facing the wall with their swim trunks slightly lowered and they were … OMGosh, I was inside the MEN'S room! I dropped my chin to my chest and all but shut my eyes, reached into the stall, grabbed Caleb's arm just as he was about to explode, and yanked him out the door. That poor child! Ron had taken him to the restroom several times already during the weekend, so Caleb naturally headed into the men's room. I was so worried about his ability to "hold it," that I didn't pay attention, I just followed him like he was my shepherd, and I was a dumb sheep.

A man was going in as we were racing out. We exchanged awkward glances. I felt like I was in a dreamlike mental slow motion. It seemed like it took a lifetime for the message in my brain to change from "What are these men doing in the ladies room?" to "What the heck am I DOING IN THE MEN'S ROOM?" UGH!™

I managed to get Caleb into the ladies restroom IN TIME, and I didn't mind that he dawdled. I actually encouraged him to amuse himself with the motion-sensory playland in the sink area. I was buying time to allow the men's room to clear out and for my red face to return to normal. How embarrassing!

I spent the rest of the weekend hiding under the protective cover of several fake palm trees and a cabana awning with my nose buried in a *People* magazine, hoping never to cross paths with those I had encountered in the men's room again.

The Public Restroom Gauntlet of Gadgets

Ask any mother of a child under five where to find a public restroom, and she could give you a half-dozen options. But she will direct you to the cleanest one that is closest to you. Ask a dad the same question, and he will scratch his head and tell you he thought he saw a port-a-potty on the side of the road a mile back. Face it, when moms (or dads, for that matter) have young ones in tow, finding the restroom can be of the utmost importance.

Twenty years ago, public restrooms were predictable. One could enter with a fair amount of confidence that you would be able to operate the basic equipment found there. You knew that once you took care of business, there would be a handle for you to place your hand on to flush the toilet. You could count on there being enough water and force initiated from pushing that handle that IT would actually go down.

You could count on a sink with two more handles—one for hot water and one for cold. You would turn these handles to make the water come out, and then turn them again to shut the water off—righty tighty, lefty loosey. Simple!

Likely, there would be yet another small handle that you would turn to crank out some paper towel to dry your hands. Or, there would be a large loop of white cotton fabric that would hang down in a long ring that you could pull on to find a clean spot to use. (I never did like those. They look too much like old men's underwear—a suppressed memory from my childhood, I'm sure.)

Public restrooms are totally different today. What we now have is the result of think tanks full of environmental engineers who have gotten together to invent ways to make our public washroom experiences more "green" and hands-free and thus more challenging. Good luck finding a handle anywhere. Everything is on some sort of motion sensor.

When you get up from the "throne," it's supposed to sense that and automatically flush. Get up the wrong way and you'll end up waving your arms like a New Yorker trying to flag down a cab driver during rush hour in a two-foot by two-foot cubicle.

I've been caught numerous times and have witnessed others in a state of bewilderment trying to maneuver the basics in the ladies room. As soon as I become accustomed to hand waving to turn on the water, I come across a restroom with faucets that don't have motion sensors, but rather buttons that you push. I have done a fair amount of waving at sinks all for naught.

I have also been guilty of leaving a faucet on and walking away because I thought it had one of those automatic off switches. It didn't, and the geniuses who thought this would save water were wrong!

One time, I went into the restroom at a carwash/oil change place. I opened the door and an overhead light went on. *Ah*, I thought. *That's neat*, and for a moment, I wished I had about ten of those for every room in my house. But, I use the technology of "common sense" at home. I cut back on our electricity bill by unscrewing lightbulbs. The light fixtures in the bedrooms of my home take two bulbs. I simply unscrew one of them. Since my boys don't bother to tighten them and my husband doesn't care to change them, we're good. No fancy sensors required.

So, I went into the restroom at the carwash and the light went on, and I was in there doing my thing. Suddenly, and quite unexpectedly, the light went off. There I sat in total darkness.

"Oh, that is just great," I said out loud for no one to hear. "Now I have to pee in the dark."

Moments later, the light went back on, and it was a good thing because the toilet wouldn't flush without sensing motion. All it sensed with the lights out was a total eclipse.

I also needed the light to create a shadow across the sensor of the sink to get the water to start. A few waves, and it did. I washed quickly and scooted out of there while I still had "daylight." It was a good thing I didn't have one of my kids with me at the time. You put a small boy in a public restroom and make him pee in the dark, and you've got a biohazard cleanup job on your hands!

One time I walked into the public restroom of a medical office building and a woman wearing traditional female Muslim attire walked in behind me. I held the door for her, and she grinned and said, "Thanks." It was a two-stall ladies room. I went into one and she took the other. All of a sudden, I hear "Hi," followed by silence from the woman. I was taken aback, but what the heck, I said "Hello?" back. I didn't want to be rude, although I found it awkward to be exchanging niceties with a total stranger while using the restroom. But perhaps that was quite common in her culture. I didn't know. Then there was a long uncomfortable silence followed by a string of sentences in a foreign tongue that I knew not. Apparently, this woman was talking to someone on her cell phone and NOT to me.

I hurried to get out of there before she came out of the stall. I skipped the waving with the water and the towels, and took my chances with my unclean hands (something I NEVER do). I would wash them in my own house where I knew how to use all the equipment.

I think it would be fun to have a game show where people have to make their way through an obstacle course of various bathroom apparatus as fast as they can. It could be called "Heads-Up," and hosted by Homer Simpson. That would be funny.

IT Almost Gives Grandpa a "Grabber"

Okay, I admit, I own a fake poop. It looks like the real deal, and I bought it at Riley's Trick Shop. I couldn't resist. It was near the checkout counter, and I impulsively added it to my eighties mullet wig and T-shirts that I was buying for Ron and myself. We were getting ready to go out of town for a business conference. The company was celebrating their twentieth anniversary, and since they opened for business in 1988, they were having an eighties-themed party. My dad was coming from out of town to watch the boys for a few days while we were away.

When I got home, I went into the bathroom with the "log of laughs" and placed IT on the side of the toilet seat. I came out and in my acting debut, I summoned Joel, my eleven-year-old, to come to the rescue.

"Joel, look what your brother did!"

"Mom, that is disgusting," Joel said.

"I will give you fifty bucks if you clean it up. I am not touching that thing," I said.

I knew Joel was still saving for an Xbox 360. He was like a typical Illinois politician—he could be "bought." Besides, eleven-year-olds have to take work when they can get it, so I knew I could hook him.

"*UGH!*™ Mom, wait, let me take a deep breath." He stepped out of the bathroom and into the hallway, sucked in a big gulp of oxygen, and then he went back in to face the "monster turd." I found this hilarious since the fake poop actually smelled like a rubber tire. He pulled a long piece of toilet paper off the roll and was inching closer to IT when I stepped in.

"Oh, forget it," I said, as I quickly grabbed the toilet paper out of his hand and used it to pick IT up. Then I threw IT at Joel and he jumped back and screamed, "Mom, are you crazy?" I started laughing as IT bounced off the tile floor, and of course, he realized that I GOT HIM.

After that, Joel carefully calculated four different ways to trick all four of his brothers. It was fun to watch each of the boys get "taken" by the poop prop.

Before Ron and I left for our trip, I gave the poop to Joel and said, "Here, get Grandpa when he's here. You guys will have fun with that."

"Okay, Mom," Joel said.

My dad used what I call "colorful language." He worked on construction sites most of his life as a union laborer, and let's just say that he didn't mince words. Well, when Joel set up the gag for Grandpa (who also has an extremely weak stomach), my dad fell for IT and put together an impressive string of expletives in front of the kids. Caleb, who was six at the time, let us know (along with his kindergarten teacher) that "Grandpa Butch swears when he gets mad." We reminded Caleb not to repeat those things—especially at school and in church. Now I just hope that the boys won't get the idea to "fake" me out with a "real" deal. That would show me.

"IT" Survival Tips

What can I say? I live with six guys, so I've succumbed to the reality that IT is going to be a part of my existence. Here is what swimming in a testosterocean for twenty years has taught me about IT:

1. Discussions about IT aren't off limits at the dinner table, in a small car, or under the covers, but they should be!

2. The human male seems to find uncommon joy in announcing IT, talking about IT, and even reminiscing about IT.

3. We would all be miserable without IT.

4. Men make a big deal about IT.

5. Women would rather not acknowledge IT.

6. Mom ends up cleaning IT, and that is when IT really hits the fan!

7. Some people find IT hard to let go of in public, while others (unfortunately) seem to have no problem whatsoever.

8. Tough guys DON'T TAKE ANY OF IT from anybody.

9. When you are the target of a practical joke involving IT, IT is not funny.

10. IT is always better OUT than IN. Well, at least that's what Shrek said.

(On a side note, I have learned to laugh about IT and that has made IT tolerable.)

Chapter Six

The Laughter Came After

Fire in the Hole

It's been scientifically proven that multitasking is counterproductive. It's also downright dangerous. I have been quite literally burned by the multitasking myth many times. Countless cookies have ended up at the bottom of my garbage can because I was doing laundry in between batches.

One time, my husband nearly torched our kitchen when he decided to hop in the shower while two loaves of butter-soaked garlic bread lay faceup four inches from the broiler set on HIGH. As usual, we had kids everywhere that day, and I put the bread in and told Ron to keep an eye on it while I went to pick up our pizzas. Don't ask me how he thought he was going to be able to do that from the shower.

Thankfully, God has given our family at least one level-head of calm. Our oldest son, Nate, was just about ten years old when this happened, and he doesn't get too rattled about anything. He's kind of the "Eeyore" in our household. He's comfortable on the sidelines and doesn't like to bring attention to himself. Nate knocked on the bathroom door and said, "Um, Dad, I think you better come to the kitchen now. The oven is on fire." THE GARLIC BREAD, Ron remembered and he threw something on and trotted out to the kitchen to put out the fire.

As I turned the corner on our street with two piping hot pizzas sitting next to me, I could see smoke coming out of the front of our house. The front door was wide-open. I parked in the garage and came in through the kitchen, where Ron had the back door open too. Our five children were lined up like the old-time fire brigade waving place mats and paper plates trying to get the smoke to clear the house.

That was the inaugural fire in our oven, but others followed. One Thanksgiving, I was having the family over for the "big bird" celebration and there were quite a few people coming. I had a twenty-pound turkey in my oven that I had swooned over for what seemed like an eternal courtship—baste, baste, baste—that bird and I had bonded. There were several side dishes vying for my affection, but none captured my fancy as much as that turkey.

Mr. Turkey took up the top rack and most of the oven space. I had a sweet potato casserole on the lower rack and a green bean casserole next to that. I wanted to make corn casserole using a new recipe I had gotten from a friend. I read the instructions and combined the canned corn with two boxes of corn bread mix and lots and lots of butter and sour cream. (This was not a friend from my Weight Watchers group.) I only had about a ten-inch-square spot left in the oven, so I scraped the corn mixture into an eight-by-eight glass baking dish and placed it next to the green beans.

My impressive Thanksgiving feast would be ready in about a half hour. The family would be walking through the door any minute, and I was pleased with myself because it looked like I had finally mastered the great art of getting the whole meal to come out at the same time. There were plenty of previous holidays where we either said "forget it" and ordered Pizza Hut, or we ate the potatoes with dessert. This time, everything was going to be perfect.

I busied myself with last-minute details. I made sure that the real butter was at the adult table and the giant tub of spread was at the kiddie table. I put croutons on the salad and jammed two salad forks into the bowl. I lifted the lid on my Crockpot to smell the stuffing. My glasses fogged for a moment as the aroma of sage, buttered onions, and spices made my mouth water. The doorbell rang and I wiped my glasses, hung the kitchen towel on the oven handle, and answered the door.

My dad and my sister and her husband came in carrying desserts and appetizers. We exchanged hugs and my nephew Ben zoomed passed us to find my boys. I reached out and grabbed the tail end of his hockey jersey and forced a hug for Aunt Tracy while Ben rolled his eyes. My niece Shana gave me a voluntary hug.

Just as we shut the door, my mother-in-law, Paula, and her husband, Jack, pulled into the driveway. She came in carrying dinner rolls and some treats for the boys. Jack followed with a case of bottled water and a bottle of wine.

Jack was similar in nature to Nate. He was a quiet observer of life and nothing much seemed to rattle his cage. With all the hustle and bustle of kids zipping around the house, the doorbell, and finding room on top of the washer and dryer for desserts, I totally lost track of time and sure enough, the house was starting to fill with smoke.

"I smell smoke," Jack said. "Is something on fire?"

"Don't be silly," I said. "What could be on fire?"

"Where there's smoke, there's fire," he said.

Sure enough, my oven was ON FIRE. Apparently, the eight-inch-square pan that housed that stupid corn casserole wasn't big enough. It needed to be put in a larger pan because the corn bread mix made it expand. (Pan size was not indicated on the recipe—thank you very much.) That expansion pushed the stick of butter over the sides, which started a grease fire in the bottom of my oven.

Ron opened the oven door and Paula corralled all the kids safely in the living room. Jack grabbed a fire extinguisher that was mounted on the wall in my laundry room. He was about to pull the pin and start spraying.

"STOP!!!" I yelled. There was NO WAY I was going to sacrifice my turkey as a burnt offering for a little thing like a fire. I rolled up my sleeves and put extra-long silver-gray oven mitts on both hands. I reached in and grabbed the handles of the turkey's roasting pan. I quickly rescued the bird and set it on top of the stove.

I didn't care as much about the corn, green beans, and sweet potatoes, but luckily, Ron was able to get them out of there and throw a little baking soda on the flames. We didn't need the fire extinguisher after all.

Ron's sister, Danette, walked through our open front door and said, "Why is the front door wide-open?" She took one look at our charred oven and realized that we had a little extra excitement getting our turkey cooked. "Are we ordering pizza AGAIN?" she asked with a grin.

"NO! I salvaged dinner this time, but we were seconds away from looking for a Pizza Hut that is open on Thanksgiving Day!"

I'd say that the Thanksgiving meal was a success. The turkey was delicious and the corn casserole had just a hint of smokey flavor. The afternoon ended with the usual football marathon on TV, with Grandpa napping on the recliner, and kids racing around the house with their endless energy. I made sure to make a note on my corn casserole recipe card: "AVOID FIRE, USE A 9X13 PAN!"

It's Ten O'Clock, Do You Know Where Your Children Are?

My grandma Rose didn't get her driver's license until she was over fifty years old. She and Grandpa Joe lived in a small town in Illinois where he walked to work every day, and she walked to the post office to buy a stamp or to Dean's Hardware to pick up a mousetrap. Al Plantan was the only grocer in town, and he took orders daily and delivered them in his pickup truck.

My grandparents weren't the only ones to live without a mode of transportation. They were a part of that "greatest generation" of people who made the world a better place because they lived with less. There were plenty of others getting along in the same way. Even without a driver in the family, my mother and her brother were active in school activities and went on to become successful adults.

Wow! How did they become educated, well-rounded, thinking people without having their parents cart them around like chickens with their heads cut off to half a dozen sporting practices during the week, topped off with out-of-state road trips on the weekends for travel teams?

We currently have four drivers in our household and three vehicles (one is usually out of gas, or in need of an oil change, or air in the tire, so actually, I would say that we have two vehicles at our disposal at any given time). Even with that many options for drivers, we still have trouble figuring out how everyone in our busy household is going to get dropped off and picked up at the right time.

One time I was going and my husband was coming. I left for an evening meeting for work before Ron got home. I dropped off Joel, who was about ten years old at the time, at C.J.'s house. C.J. lived in our neighborhood. I told the other boys where I was going and that I was dropping Joel off and that Dad would be home soon.

When I came back from my meeting, it was late and since it was a school night, Adam and Caleb were in bed sleeping. I went to their rooms to tuck them in, and I peeked into Nate's and Luke's rooms to say goodnight to them as well. Then I got the feeling that something was missing or that I was forgetting something. It hit me. Joel wasn't home!

The doors to our bedrooms are all in a row upstairs. Joel's room was actually a closet. He was sick of sharing a room, so we cleared out the closet room next to my bedroom and put his bed in there. He had a door and a window and enough room for his bed and little else. The space was supposed to be my walk-in Master Closet, but I didn't really need it. I certainly didn't need a whole room for my unimpressive collection of one pair of jeans that actually fit and several "skinny" jeans that I'd never wear again.

I looked in the closet/room, and Joel wasn't there. He certainly couldn't hide or get lost in there. I actually started to get concerned.

"Where's Joel?" I asked Ron.

"I haven't seen him since I got home," he said.

Hmmm, I thought, that was three hours ago. It was nearly 10 p.m. and well past bedtime on a school night. "Is he STILL at C.J.'s?" I asked.

"I didn't know he was at C.J.'s," Ron said.

I tried to call C.J.'s mom. No answer. *UGH!*™ "I'm going over there," I said as I put my coat and shoes back on and went back out the door. Sure enough, Joel was at C.J.'s playing video games. C.J. had showered and was in his pajamas. His mom and dad had gone to bed and the boys were playing Xbox in the living room.

"Why didn't you just come home, Joel?" I asked. C.J. lived down the street and Joel could have walked home easily.

"I don't know," Joel said. "I was just playing video games."

"Good night, C.J., and thanks for having Joel. See you tomorrow," I said and we left.

I talked to C.J.'s mom later, and we laughed about it. She said she knew we would eventually realize we were missing a kid. She said she had tried to call us, but got no answer.

That wasn't as bad as the time that Ron and I both thought that our son Luke was getting a ride home from someone else. Luke was in junior high and on the track team. He had a meet that was out of town, and I thought that my car-pool partner, Pam, was bringing Luke home along with her daughter Jackie. Turned out that Pam and Jackie were out of town and not going to the meet at all. I incorrectly assumed that Luke had a way to get home.

Once again, Ron was zigging while I was zagging and we missed each other. I had another evening meeting, and he wasn't home yet from work. So we didn't touch base. In addition to that, our phone was on the blink. Luke was using someone's cell phone to call us, but couldn't get through.

I came home and noticed that Luke was gone. "Where's Luke?" I asked. No one knew. I called Pam on her cell phone and that was when the panic set in.

"Pam, do you have Luke?" I asked her.

"No," she said and she sounded surprised. "Jackie didn't go to the meet today because we are out of town."

My stomach did a flip and my heart skipped a beat. "Okay, I'll find him," I said.

I put my coat and shoes back on and went back out the door. I was going to head over to the junior high to see if he was there. Headlights were pulling into my driveway just as I shut the door behind me. It was Sherry, another mom whose son was a friend of Luke's. Luke waited at the school until all the other kids had been picked up. It was just he and Coach left. Since he couldn't get in touch with us, he called his friend's mom.

A flood of emotions from relief, guilt, appreciation, and embarrassment ran through me all at once. I thanked Sherry for her help. She was so gracious and understanding. Her son wasn't even on the team. She had to drive out to the school from home just to get Luke. As soon as we got into the house, I apologized to Luke for the mix-up. I explained what happened and while he wasn't mad, he started to cry a little. He was scared about being left at the school and embarrassed.

I quit going to meetings in the evening, and we have gotten better about making sure the boys are accounted for each night. I have a "system" now. Before I double-check to make sure that everything is locked up for the night, I look at the pile of stuff by the front door and make sure there are five pairs of smelly tennis shoes. On weekends, I often find an extra pair or two as my boys regularly invite friends to spend the night. That is fine. As long as there are at least five pairs there, we're good.

Footprints in Wet Cement (Not so inspiring!)

"Ron?" I blubbered through real tears while clutching the phone with both hands to my ear.

"What's the matter?" my husband asked.

He was at work and I was home with the boys. My voice climbed higher, and I blurted out, "I HATE THESE KIDS!" My crying turned to mild sobbing. Ron and I had been saving money for several months for a service walkway along the side of our garage. We also needed a flat place to keep our garbage cans. We were all set to have a concrete slab poured, along with a nice sidewalk. The work was to be done by our friend Bill, a concrete contractor whom we have known for many years. We attended the same church.

Bill and his crew had come out the day before to set up the forms. The cement truck was scheduled for first thing the next morning. It was a warm summer day, and my boys were up and about early when the truck pulled up to our house. I made sure that everyone was accounted for and safely on the front porch while Bill's crew got ready to pour.

All little boys love to watch construction machinery. This day was no exception. I not only had my five boys in the peanut gallery, but our neighbor boy C.J. as well. Two men with rubber boots and canvas gloves adjusted the long metal shoot that would deliver the wet cement into the forms. Bill grabbed a tricycle and plastic Easter bucket with a broken handle out of the designated sidewalk area. I guess the boys were playing there the day before. I apologized for the stuff being in the way, but Bill was especially patient and understanding.

"Don't worry about it," he said. Bill had three boys of his own and two of them matched two of ours in age, so our families had shared many "boy-ventures" together. In fact, Bill's driveway was where my son Luke busted open his chin and then needed his second round of stitches. Bill also came from a family of seven children—six of them BOYS! He definitely was not someone who required a "boys will be boys" explanation. He lived it as a kid and was living it again as a dad.

The men continued their work and in short order, the new sidewalk and slab for our garbage cans was finished. I thanked Bill and his guys and couldn't wait for it to dry so I could easily roll our garbage cans into their new spot.

I asked Bill if the cement was set enough to have the boys put their handprints in the corner of the slab.

"Sure," he said, "but you're going to want to do it quick. This stuff sets up fast." Bill and his crew gathered up their tools and left for their next job.

I called all the boys over and started lining them up according to age. I even put C.J. in the mix, since he had become a regular at our house. We would have six handprints in the corner. I helped each one place his hand into the wet cement and Bill was right, it was setting up fast. I got to the sixth boy and realized that Caleb was nowhere to be found. Caleb was just over two years old at the time. He had meandered into the backyard and around to the other side of the house.

"CALEB," I called as I finished pressing my son Adam's hand into the cement. The other boys were washing their hands with the hose in the front of the house.

"CALEB," I called again, but louder. Caleb had made his way to the front yard and was sticking his hands into the stream of water while the other boys cleaned up. This time, he heard me. He ran toward my voice and before I knew it, Caleb was impressing a dozen evenly spaced images of the bottom of his big chunky toddler sandals into my freshly poured sidewalk.

I shot up from my crouched position and yanked Adam's hand out of the cement. "WHAT ARE YOU DOING?" I screamed. Caleb had no clue. Of course he didn't. He was only two, and he couldn't possibly understand what sacrifices his mommy and daddy made in order to save up for the sidewalk. He certainly couldn't understand what a pain in the rump it was to store our garbage cans on an uneven piece of ground that was always mud-saturated in the spring.

And, furthermore, he couldn't be expected to understand the science behind cement and how it works. All he knew was that he heard his mommy's voice calling his name.

Even though the "Mommy Dearest" side of me wanted to grab Caleb and shake him, I knew it wasn't his fault. I sent all the boys inside and pulled my cell phone out of my pocket. That was when I called Ron. After I told him what happened, he told me to call Bill and ask him if he could come back and smooth it out. I felt bad because I knew that Bill and his guys were headed to another job. I called him anyway.

Bill came back alone while his guys went on ahead. It was obvious that I had been crying. Bill smiled and reassured me that it was no problem. He grabbed a finishing tool from the metal toolbox in the back of his truck and went to work stretching over the sidewalk to reach Caleb's footprints. The cement had set to a point where Bill could mostly even things out, but if you look close, you can still see where little Caleb left his "footprints in the sand."

Ron said it would have been funny to just leave the footprints in there. I saw no humor in that and reminded Ron that while he was at work for eight to ten hours a day, I was at home with a houseful of boys and losing my mind! He shut his mouth and hugged me.

Brain Damaged Teen-age Boys Pool Vaulting

Installing an aboveground swimming pool was both one of the best and one of the worst decisions Ron and I have made. I am on a first-name basis with "Julie the Pool Chemical Expert" at my local pool supply store. When the water is crystal clear and the boys are entertained and not fighting and having a blast in the pool, it is the best idea I've ever had. When we have a thirty-thousand-gallon cesspool of algae to deal with that will take six hundred dollars worth of chemicals to clean up (not to mention countless hours of time), it's the stupidest idea Ron has ever come up with.

I've weighed the pros and cons and have decided that the pool stays! I know that Ron would like to get in his Bobcat and "accidentally" knock the thing over, but he's not the one who is left to manage the boys over summer break. So, we are keeping the pool until the "con" side gets a little more "con-ish."

There was one time when even I was ready to "throw in the towel" on the pool. Nate and Luke had a bunch of their teenage friends over for a swim party. There were seven teenagers plus Joel, Adam, and Caleb, and two of their friends, all in my thirty-foot round pool. It looked like a crowded public beach. I didn't really care as long as no one was drowning, and everyone was out of the house.

I was inside enjoying the quiet and trying to catch up on laundry (an endless task). I was also trying to get the kitchen cleaned up. Our pool sits nicely off to the side of our back deck, and I can keep an eye on the kids from our kitchen window.

I looked out and noticed that they were starting to form a whirlpool. It brought back memories of me and my brother and sister swimming at my uncle Denny's house when we were kids. We made whirlpools all the time and played Marco/Polo and dove for pennies that Uncle Denny would throw into the water.

My nostalgic trip down memory lane was disrupted when I noticed that the whirlpool the boys were creating was causing the pool ladder, which was attached to the deck, to heave up and down. It looked like it would snap. I cranked open the kitchen window to yell "KNOCK IT OFF!!"

The dryer dinged, and that was my signal to switch loads. I cranked the kitchen window shut and spent the next several minutes folding clothes, figuring out which underwear belonged to which kid, and putting them into the seven baskets that I had on deep shelves next to my washing machine.

It is next to impossible to keep five boys in decent-looking and clean clothes!

I put the wet clothes in the dryer and started it. Then, yet another dirty load went into the washer. I knew I had at least an hour or so before I had to repeat that process, so I decided it would be a great time to grab a Diet Coke and a magazine and relax for a few moments.

I walked into the kitchen and opened the refrigerator door to get some ice. In my peripheral vision, I could see a fifteen-foot long metal pole sticking out of my pool, with boys taking turns catapulting themselves into the air. I cranked the kitchen window back open and screamed for everybody to get out of the pool. Our pool had a plastic liner. Applying force from a metal object to any type of plastic usually will result in the plastic needing to be replaced.

"ARE YOU BRAIN-DAMAGED?" I yelled to my oldest son, Nate. "You are going to rip the liner that way. Get out, get out, get out!" I cranked the window shut once more. I couldn't believe it. The boys got out of the pool and dried off. I sent everyone from whom I was not getting a tax deduction to their own homes. I lectured my boys about proper pool behavior and how now "Dad might get his wish and just tear down the pool with his Bobcat."

I called Ron at work. "I HATE THESE KIDS!" He'd heard that before. I told him what happened. Ron listened to me and said, "It's not that bad. It's just a liner. We'll get it fixed. At least you're not calling me to tell me someone got hurt, or God forbid, drowned in the pool. That would be really bad. This is just kinda bad." He had a point.

Only time would tell if there was a hole or not. The next morning I glanced out the kitchen window while filling the coffeepot with water and my fears were confirmed: yep, we were losing water. The pool was down about two feet. We had to empty it and have the liner replaced. It took several days to drain the water, remove the liner and replace it, and refill the pool with water. It was a good thing that we could pump the remaining water out of the pool and into the drainage ditch around our yard or we would have had one heck of a mud puddle. But, eventually, the pool was once again my "sanity savior" as it entertained countless boys on hot summer days.

Sergeant Mom Gets the Morning MOVE! MOVE! MOVING!

Routines make the world go around. Businesses manufacture products and get them to consumers using routines. Schools educate young minds using routines. The entire United States military is one giant routine "machine." Families are no different. Families function best with routines— just ask Supernanny. Being the mother of a large family has forced me into the whole routine mode. My nature is very spontaneous and carefree, but that doesn't bode well when one must see to it that five children make it to four different schools on time and with something that resembles a lunch while I make it to work by 8:30.

My routine adaptation looked a lot like Sergeant Carter from the *Gomer Pyle* sitcom. MOVE! MOVE! MOVE! It was my morning mantra. Over the years, I have been known to stir the children on a school day using a variety of methods. Yes, I own a referee's whistle and am not afraid to use it. Yes, I have used the mist button on my iron (cool iron, of course) to spray a sleepy teenage face into the land of the living. And, I have been know to call a cell phone and even use a text message to wake up my son Joel. He thought I was one of his friends—HA!

I'll never forget one particularly chaotic morning when it seemed all of my efforts were failing. The boys were in slow motion, and I was on HIGH ALERT. I had to be at work on time for a meeting, so I pulled out all the stops.

"Adam, get your lunch! Joel, where's your backpack? Caleb, get your shoes! Nate, start the car. Luke, brush your teeth! Come on people, MOVE! MOVE! MOVE!!!" I made it out of the subdivision with just enough time left to drop off Caleb at preschool and get to work on time. I pulled into the lot of his school and left my car running. I opened the slider door of my minivan and unbuckled Caleb's car seat.

"Hurry up, Cae," I said while I tugged a knit hat over his ears. It was a chilly fall day. I held onto Caleb's hand and yanked him up the stairs to the front door of the preschool. There was a dad standing in the middle of the doorway dressed in a suit and tie with a dark-colored overcoat. He held the door open with his backside and was trying to get his daughter to say, "Bye-bye."

My thoughts were racing well in front of me, and when I came upon the dad in the doorway, I physically stopped, but my brain kept moving. My mouth kept moving too as I barked at the man, "IN or OUT?" He turned his head to see what kind of rude intrusion had just interrupted his ritualistic morning "good-bye" ceremony with his daughter. Instantly, I snapped out of the trance that I was in, and I gasped and covered my mouth with my right hand as if I had just let a swear word slip in front of the pope. I had just treated a well-dressed grown man like he was a subordinate.

"Oh my gosh, sir, I am so very sorry! You are looking at the face of crazy right here," I said, as made a circle with my index finger around my face. "See, I have five children, and they are ALL BOYS, and I have to get them out the door by eight every day, all by myself," and yatta yatta yatta.

He smiled and moved himself "IN" and stepped to the side as I came through with Caleb. I could see that my explanation wasn't going to compensate for my actions, so I quit trying to justify my behavior. I gave Caleb a quick kiss and signed the attendance sheet and went to the office.

I was working part-time for my church, which was only blocks away from the preschool. I was on time for my meeting, and the Sunday that followed, I was in charge of giving the announcements from the pulpit before the church services started. It was my job to help visitors get connected with other members. Moments before it was time for me to go up to the microphone, I scanned the crowd in the sanctuary.

"Dear Lord," I prayed, "forgive me for my attitude this week, and PLEASE don't let that man in the suit at the preschool visit THIS church on THIS day. Please, Holy Spirit, send him to the nice Baptist church down the road where there are no crazy mothers of five boys who scold perfectly grown adults for lingering in a doorway trying to get their daughter to say BYE-BYE!" Amen.

Thankfully, God answered my prayer and I didn't see the man that day. I carefully avoided him at the preschool on the mornings that followed, hoping to just forget about it. And from that day forward, I have tried to leave my "Sergeant Carter" impersonation at home.

Survival Tips for Those Days When Nothing is Funny

In the heat of the moment, when everything is falling apart, it's critical for moms to maintain a proper perspective. My husband helps me with his "it's only a car, a pool, and a sidewalk" speeches. So here are just a few tips that will hopefully help you when you are ABOUT TO LOSE IT!

1. Leave the room. I've done this many times and it really helps. Physical separation from the chaos is necessary so you can sort out your emotions. Once you calm down and have processed it a little, then go back and deal with it.

2. Leave the house. I've done this too! I am a huge fan of humor-
    ous greeting cards and there have been many times that I have
    passed the parenting baton to Ron while I spent an hour at the
    grocery store reading every humorous card on the shelves. It's
    very inexpensive therapy!

3. Be gracious. Giving grace to another human being is one of the
    most benevolent things we can do for each other. It's an expres-
    sion of understanding that we all make mistakes. When you are
    having a bad day, be extra gracious and you will find that your
    day improves significantly.

4. Be forgiving. When we forgive another, we extend a hand of
    love to the offending party and we bring a blessing on our own
    soul as we heal from that offense. Forgiveness is an absolute ne-
    cessity for all people.

5. Remember that this season in life will pass. My husband was
    right about the footprints in the cement. Now that several years
    have passed, I do wish the mini-footprints were still there. Our
    kids grow up so fast, but on *those* days, it feels like we are in an
    El Nino.

6. Stay connected with your gal pals. Moms need moms! We need
    that female bond of sisterhood that strengthens our founda-
    tion and our ability to cope. Keep your gal pals close and call on
    them when you need help.

7. Keep saying, "It could be worse!" Any situation could be worse.
    So whatever you are experiencing, think about it in the worse
    possible scenario and then give thanks that IT'S NOT THAT BAD!
    This sounds a little crazy, but it works.

8. Be thankful for all the little things in life. So often we focus on the
    things in our lives that get us down while overlooking our many
    blessings. One summer when I was going through a very diffi-
    cult season in motherhood, I kept a daily journal of appreciation. I
    wrote down every little thing in my life that I was giving thanks for
    and it really helped. I was thankful for running water, Chapstick,

and clean pajamas. The key is to get your eyes off the things that bother you and on the things that make you smile! ;o)

9. Pamper yourself and don't feel guilty about it. Mom, you are the glue of your family. You are the kingpin. You are the hub. Take care of YOU. Treat yourself with the same love and care that you treat others. Put yourself on your priority list.

10. Laugh at yourself! Did you know that it is impossible to laugh while holding an angry thought? It's true. So in the words of my teenagers, "CHILLAX!" Don't take life so seriously. Have fun! Play with your kids. Enjoy having a child in your life by allowing yourself the freedom to be like one.

Chapter Seven

I've Got the Joy Joy Joy Joy

It was another Monday and my morning shower was interrupted by pounding on the door. It was my eight-year-old, Adam.

"Mom!!! Come quick. Joel and Caleb are dying!!! HURRY!!!" His tone was undeniable.

Why is it that every time I get undressed, someone in my house WANTS me? Either one of the kids wants to tell me how it was Vespucchi and not Columbus who discovered America, or my husband *wants* me which is how we ended up with so many kids in the first place! I hurried to get a robe and barely had it tied around my waist as I opened the door with shampoo still in my hair and said, "WHHHH-HAT?"

"Mom, I'm serious," Adam said. "Joel and Caleb are both crying to DEATH."

I went into Caleb's bedroom and found him sitting on the floor balling, with his legs crossed. He had a fearful look in his eyes and when I looked at his right hand, I could see why. Caleb was six years old and a forever curious boy. He had a wrench stuck on his finger. It wouldn't come off. The harder Caleb tugged on the wrench, the more his finger tugged back.

A "jump on the bed" contest had ensued in the boys' bedroom the night before and my husband had to tighten up the guardrail on the top bunk. Ron apparently left his tools on the dresser, because Caleb took Daddy's wrench and stuck it on his finger. What possesses boys to do these kinds of things?

Joel was crying too, but his crying seemed less panicked at the moment, so I made a "triage" decision and treated the loudest crier first. I told Caleb that I was sure I could get it off. "Come with me," I said and I took him into the bathroom. I took his hand and put it under cool water. I could feel the tension in his shoulder and patted it and said, "It's okay, Caleb! I'm gonna put some soap on your hand and it should slip right off."

"Is it going to hurt?" he looked up at me and asked with both shoulders back in the "up" position. His blue eyes still had real tears, although the screaming had subsided.

"No, you won't feel…" By the time I finished explaining the procedure to him, I had the thing off. Such an ordeal! I told him to hurry up and get ready for school.

Joel was still crying, so I went to find out what was the matter. "Mom, my ankle hurts really bad," he said. I hit the rewind button in my brain and remembered that Joel was also in on the jumping escapade on the bunk beds the night before.

"You probably sprained it last night when you guys were goofing around," I told him. "Now, get up and get ready for school." I walked out of the room and went back to the shower to rinse the shampoo out of my hair. A few minutes later, I was dressed and making coffee.

"Mom, Joel is really going to die!" Adam said.

"Adam, Joel is fine. He just twisted his ankle and you know my rule—if you do not have a fever or did not throw up, YOU GO TO SCHOOL!" I said. If I let the boys stay home for every time I've heard, "I don't feel good. My stomach hurts. I have a sore throat. My ear hurts," I would be raising complete idiots because they would never be in school. So, that is why I came up with the fever/puke criteria. It was either that or invest eight thousand dollars in a polygraph machine.

Joel got himself dressed and hopped on one foot down the stairs. He had stopped crying, but he wouldn't put any weight on his ankle. I was busy making lunches and getting myself ready for work and wasn't paying much attention to Joel. Nate and Luke were old enough to make sure they had themselves ready, but they were in desperate need of a swift kick in the pants on that morning. I was happy to oblige.

The first bus was going to come around the corner at any minute. "Joel, Adam, Caleb, BUS!!!!" I screamed. Adam and Caleb came running and grabbed their backpacks, lunches, and coats and flew down the driveway. Joel was gimping along, still hopping on one foot.

"Joel, just walk it out," I said.

"I can't Mom," he said.

"Okay, forget it. I will drive you to school, but you ARE GOING!" Half of me thought he was faking it, and the other half wondered if he had a fracture. ALL of me was certain that the origin of the pain was a direct result of "boys being boys" and the horsing around they were doing the night before on the bunk beds.

Adam and Caleb got on their bus, and Nate and Luke took the second bus minutes later. I told Joel to get his stuff and meet me in the van. I threw a Lean Cuisine in my bag for lunch and couldn't find my keys. A few minutes of searching and I found them on the island in the kitchen under a bunch of Adam's school papers.

Joel was waiting in the front passenger's seat of my mini-van. He seemed fine to me; he just refused to walk on his ankle. We drove the mile and a half to Green Garden Elementary. It was early spring and a cold, wet, and windy day. I intentionally parked my car in the farthest space available in the lot, figuring that Joel would eventually give up on his hopping-on-one-leg routine.

Well, he didn't. Halfway through the parking lot, he fell to the ground and cried believable tears that convinced me that he had a real problem, and he wasn't faking it. I felt terrible! We were halfway between the van and the building, so I decided to give Joel a piggyback ride into the school so we could figure out what to do from there. It must've been a sight with me fighting the wind and struggling to keep his long and lanky body off the ground. He was almost ten years old at the time and we were well past the piggyback stage.

The school nurse was in the office when we finally got into the building. I told her about Joel's ankle and she sat him down to take a look. She ran him through a series of instructions like wiggle this and that, and does it hurt when I do this and that, but she, of course, advised us to take him to our family doctor.

I called the doctor, and he told us to come right over to his office. He took an X-ray of Joel's ankle. It didn't show a fracture. It wasn't a bone issue. The pain seemed to be in Joel's joints. The doctor wanted us to see a rheumatology specialist to run tests for arthritis. He recommended one and we made an appointment for the end of the week.

Joel had been diagnosed with strep throat a few weeks earlier, and he had completed a full course of antibiotics. As it turns out (I did not know this), you can get a temporary form of arthritis from a strep infection. What I thought was a case of "I don't feel like going to school because I twisted my ankle horsing around like a ding dong with my brothers syndrome" ended up being *post-streptococcal reactive arthritis,* and we found ourselves at the beginning of a two-and-a-half-year journey.

When the specialist told us that Joel had arthritis and that he would have to be on an antibiotic for an extended period of time to prevent permanent damage to his heart valves, I really felt bad that I made him walk halfway across the school parking lot fighting the wind and freezing rain. Talk about your guilt trips. I was on a guilt cruise and my guilt ship was adrift in a great big ocean.

We had a few roller-coaster rides during Joel's struggle with arthritis. He would be fine for a while, and then have a major flare-up. Once, he was hospitalized in severe pain. He was prescribed a variety of pain medications and had an allergic reaction to one that prompted yet another trip to the emergency room. Joel missed a lot of school in third and fourth grade.

He and I watched the St. Louis Cardinals win the World Series in 2006 from a hospital bed at Children's Memorial in Chicago. We were Sox fans, but since the Sox were out of it, we rooted for Mr. McCalister's Cardinals. Mr. McCalister was Joel's fourth grade teacher.

The worst thing in the world for a mother is to see her child suffer. There is such a feeling of helplessness and deep sorrow when you see your child hurting and you are powerless to help. Joel was a young boy who went from running around like a nut, to having the aches and pains of an elderly man. During a flare-up, he would wake up in the morning and have to crawl on his hands and knees to the bathroom and slip into a warm bath to loosen his stiff joints after a night's rest. He was in a wheelchair for a period of time and in physical therapy for months to get everything moving again. He messed up some of his healthy parts on the opposite side of his body by the natural overcompensation that would come while he tried to function and avoid pain.

On the bright side, Joel seemed to be a little more empathetic to people in pain after going through all of this. He really bonded with a man named Rich from our church who had serious health issues. Rich was praying daily for Joel's recovery and it meant a lot to Joel and to us that Rich cared so much. Joel also seemed to pay more attention to my dad who had diabetes and also struggled with pain in his back from time to time. Dad was visiting us and got up from the couch after a long afternoon of sitting and when he got to his feet, he groaned a bit. Joel said, "Don't worry, Grandpa, once you get moving again, that pain will go away. That's what happened to me."

Looking back on the whole situation with Joel, I am thankful for the experience. Many prayers were said for Joel to be out of pain and for him to get back to the normal life of a young kid—horsing around with his brothers, breaking bunk beds, and chasing girls at recess.

I hope and pray that I never have to go through an illness with a child again. I hope that I never again have to spend the night in a vinyl-covered hospital chair that sits too low to the ground and has skinny wooden arms that cut into my hips while I try to curl up into some sort of sleeping position.

I hope that I never again have to give a detailed report of my child's symptoms to nurse after nurse after soon-to-be nurse, and to doctor after doctor after soon-to-be doctor! I hope that I never have to say to my hospitalized kid, "Oh look, here comes the volunteer with his 'entertainment' cart again. What kind of coloring book would you like this time?" I never again want to take a shower in the "parent bathroom" of the peds unit. And I do not want to have to buy a T-shirt and a toothbrush from another hospital gift shop.

But since I did have to go through all of that, and since it's now OVER (thanks be to God!), I can now be thankful for all the things that Joel's illness taught me.

I once attended a conference while in college. This was long before I got married and had children, but the speaker's message stayed with me. The speaker was Mr. Le-Roy Eims of a Christian ministry called the Navigators. Mr. Eims has since passed away, but he was a tall, slim man with white hair and he was a dynamic teacher. As he spoke to our group of several hundred college students, I still can remember him saying that real lessons in life are learned in the tough times. He knew tough times.

Eims was a World War II hero, wounded in combat on September 15, 1944 during the invasion of Peleliu. His life was spared that day, while over a thousand other American lives were lost. After the war, Eims returned to the States, and like many who had fought in battle, couldn't shake the images of bloodshed he witnessed.

Eims was a nineteen-year-old Marine who was scared to death on that day—D-Day. It was something that a dying soldier asked Eims while on the battlefield and under fire that refused to leave his mind. "Do you know how to pray?" the dying soldier asked. Eims didn't. He wasn't religious.

He had never read the Bible. While those were the last words spoken for that soldier, Eims heard them over and over again long after returning home.

Troubled by the words of the dead soldier, Eims was led to buy a Bible and open a new chapter in his life. He began to read and study the Bible and it changed him forever. He went on to become a Bible teacher and author. In his presentation to our group, I remember him quoting a poem by Robert Browning Hamilton, entitled *Along the Road.*

Along the Road

By: Robert Browning Hamilton

I walked a mile with Pleasure,

She chattered all the way;

But left me none the wiser

For all she had to say.
I walked a mile with Sorrow,

And ne'er a word said she;

But oh, the things I learned from her

When Sorrow walked with me.

Somehow, I think God chose to use a very uncomfortable situation to get the attention of a terrified nineteen-year-old Marine who had never really devoted much thought to spiritual things. Somehow I don't think those words, "Do you know how to pray?" would have left such an indelible impression on Eims had they been spoken from the safety of a top bunk in a military barracks.

Even though I would never equate my crazy and chaotic life to that of a D-Day soldier in harm's way, I will say that God used my son Joel's illness to show me the joy that existed amid the chaos of raising five kids. He showed me that there is much to be celebrated along the road of parenting. He showed me that there is much to be enjoyed.

So, I've decided to mention just a few of those true joys:

1. I am joyful that spilled milk can be easily cleaned up.

2. I am joyful that each of my boys wanted to marry me at one time or another (they deny it now, but it's true).

3. I am joyful that I have been trick-or-treating nineteen consecutive years (through wind, pouring rain, sleet, and even a blizzard…okay, a light flurry, but I was there).

4. I am joyful that I take time out of a busy day to play the board game *Sorry* with Caleb.

5. I am joyful that I take time out of a busy day to snuggle with Adam and watch anything he wants on the Disney Channel.

6. I am joyful that Joel likes to have his back scratched.

7. I am joyful that Luke has good friends who like to come to our house and hang out, play football, watch football, eat everything but the football!

8. I am joyful that Nate has a wicked sense of humor, and makes us laugh.

9. I am joyful that in winter our yard is trampled with snowy footprints and snow angels, and that our entryway is littered with boots, snowpants, gloves, hats, scarves, and coats.

10. I am joyful that in the summer our yard is strewn with bikes, Frisbees, soccer balls, plastic bases, and sopping wet beach towels.

11. I am joyful that I have been on dozens of field trips with busloads of bouncing kids to places that I would have never seen if I were not a mother.

12. I am joyful that while I may have an empty fridge and a full laundry hamper, it means that my house is filled with children and there really is no greater joy. God Bless!

Afterword

How Did This Book Land in Your Hands?

My dream of becoming a writer started with *The Spartan Speaker*, a publication of DePue Junior High School. I was in sixth grade and my English teacher, Mrs. Walk (loved her), allowed a group of us to write and publish our own newspaper. We wrote fun articles and included games and puzzles in the publication, but my favorite part was printing it on the mimeograph machine in the teachers' lounge. The mimeograph was the precursor to the Xerox copier. It was very messy, but I loved the smell of the ink. It was probably a carcinogen, but what did we know back in 1978? It smelled like a million Sharpie markers, and I'm pretty sure I walked out of that lounge (no windows) at least once with a temporary buzz going.

I remember our editor, a seventh grade girl, entertained us while the mimeograph painstakingly pumped out *The Speaker*. She took long pieces of string and swallowed all but the last inch or so and then retrieved them like a magician pulling silk scarves out of a hat. We sixth graders watched in marvelous horror anticipating what would be on the end of that string once it returned from her esophagus—that is IF it returned, which was even more mesmerizing. I think we expected to see something that resembled a nightcrawler. We were disappointed every time, but she sure had a captive audience.

Our editor also stuffed herself into a metal wastebasket with just her head, feet, and hands sticking out of the top, and then she rolled around on the floor. How bizarre! She's a fancy lawyer or something like that now, which is heartening for parents of junior high students everywhere who are convinced that their child's greatest aspiration in life is to become a traveling circus performer.

Later, in high school, I wrote for *The Teen-Trib*. The high schools in my rural area were all small. There were only thirty students in my graduating class and that was a record high as most classes had a whopping fifteen to twenty-five students in them. Because of the size of the schools in our community, we published a collaborative high school newspaper called *The Teen-Trib*. Each school in the area was assigned one page, which was published weekly and distributed to subscribers of *The News Tribune*, the daily local newspaper for a dozen or so small towns. It was the only way to put something together that would give Grandma enough padding for her kitty box each week.

My major in college was journalism and public relations, and I was the editor of a weekly publication called *The Clue* during my college years. Like *The Spartan Speaker* and *The Teen- Trib*, *The Clue* was fun and entertaining, and I loved it! A year after graduating from college in 1988, I met and married my husband. Two months after the wedding, I was pregnant with son #1. I took maternity leave from my job as an administrative assistant at Joliet Junior College and while on leave, I got pregnant with son #2.

It would have cost me more than I was earning to put the boys in day care, so I resigned. I also put my writing aspirations on the "back burner," not necessarily with any real intention, but that is just sort of what happened once we started having our enormous family (also not necessarily with any real intention but just sort of what happened).

Over the years and through the woods, we've had five children—all boys. In those years, I've told hundreds of stories about our "boy-ventures" to coworkers, friends at church, and even total strangers. Oftentimes they would say to me, "You should write a book." And I have always wanted to, but never found the time. I knew I would write it one day because the things my boys have done were too funny to leave in the cobwebs of my mind. I couldn't make these things up. It's true what they say, that reality is stranger than fiction. One day, I would write THAT book!

Right before I turned forty, I, like many who find they are facing a milestone birthday, was reflective and contemplative. "What does this mean? What do I have to look forward to? What have I done? What haven't I done? Will I ever eat only half a piece of turtle cheesecake?" etc…

I didn't make a big deal about it. I was actually looking forward to forty because for me, it meant freedom. I had my fifth and final baby when I was thirty-five, so do the math. Turning forty meant that I could finally put to rest those preschool years that were tricky for sure. I was a mother of one or more preschoolers for seventeen consecutive years. That's a whole lotta sleepless nights, dirty diapers, and *Love You Forever* seemed like it would never end!

One Saturday, about two weeks before hitting the big FOUR-OH and officially climbing over that proverbial "hill," I was going about my weekend routine of cleaning. I was carrying a laundry basketful of dirty clothes from my bedroom to the laundry room. I quickly passed by a photograph of my parents that was on my dresser. The photo was taken at my wedding seventeen years earlier. I had walked past that picture countless times before, but this time was different. I stopped and looked closely at the picture of my mother. Then I looked at myself in the mirror. I looked back down at the picture of Mom and what I saw amazed me. I was looking a lot more like my mom and like a woman the age of the mother of the bride instead of looking like the bride.

I got married at the age of twenty-three, when my mom was forty-seven. At the time of my wedding, she had recently been diagnosed with terminal bone cancer. Sadly, she died at fifty-one, which meant that my mother never aged in my mind from that point.

Mom worked in the medical profession as an X-ray technician for many years while I was growing up, and when I, the youngest of her three children, was a senior in college, she quit her job at the local hospital and went back to school to become a graphic artist. She was so excited to be a middle-aged college student pursuing her dream of graphic art design. Sometimes Mom and I would study together when I was home for a visit from my campus.

At about the same time, my dad started a small promotional products distributor business as a supplement to their income. He was a full-time construction worker as a union laborer and their plan was for him to eventually retire and then they would work in the promotional products business together. Dad would do sales, and Mom would handle the art design and the office stuff.

Mom never finished her degree because she found herself facing a much bigger challenge than the pursuit of higher education and owning a business—cancer. She was diagnosed at stage three of four stages with multiple myeloma; at the time, an incurable and rare form of bone cancer. She fought like a champion for five years, but lost her life on May 29, 1993.

One of the last things that I ever did with my mom was play cards. It was only a few days before she died. There were hospice care workers coming to the house daily. Mom was confined to a hospital bed that was placed in the corner of our living room where the Christmas tree used to go. There was a small table next to the bed and a rocking chair next to that. Mom could no longer stand, sit up, or eat. She had multiple fractures in her arms, legs, and vertebrae as the cancer had deteriorated her bone. She was on regular doses of morphine for pain. We all knew that we were reading the final chapter.

When I walked in, Mom smiled and picked up a deck of cards on the table and said, "Let's play Rummy Tray. I want to do therapy with my hands." All she had left was her mind and her hands. So I shuffled the cards and tapped the deck, and we played several hands of Rummy.

Mom didn't know it, and neither did I at the time, but I would forever carry that moment with me as inspiration to do the best that I can with what I have. No one would have faulted her if she shook her fist at God and expressed anger and resentment at being forced out of the world while on the cusp of a new-found career path and the joy-filled season of grandparenting (she had four grandkids under three years old at the time). But, she never complained, never asked "Why me?" and never gave up. And even at the very end, she did the best that she could with what she had.

The real kicker was that she was cheating at Rummy. She denied it and I wondered if she was really cheating or if she didn't know she was cheating because of the morphine. The bottom line was, yep, she was cheating. I called her on it, and she just chuckled like a young schoolgirl caught with her hands in a cookie jar. She had such a great sense of humor.

When she lost all of her thick black hair because of chemotherapy, she tied a scarf to her bald head with fake bangs attached with Velcro. She used to make my three-year-old cousin giggle wildly as she let him rip her hair off then pretend that it really hurt. She was animated and a joy to be around. Kids loved her! Even the troubled boy who lived next door loved and respected my mom. This kid was plenty old enough to know better, but in an act of defiance, he peed on the floor of the kitchen in the restaurant that his parents owned. He was one of those kids that you figured you might read about in the police blotter someday. Yet, he was gentle and loving toward my mom.

So, there I stood, a near-middle aged woman with a basket of dirty laundry kind of hanging off my hip, and I realized: "WOW! I am getting pretty close to the age my mom was when she had to leave this world." That was a pivotal moment for me. It was my "Ah Ha" moment. I didn't get teary-eyed, although I have grieved and cried a river of tears over many lost moments, deeply missing my mom. I wasn't sad or depressed or feeling sorry for myself because I don't have her here. I just matter-of-factly looked at my almost forty-year-old self in the mirror and said out loud: "I am writing THAT book!" I decided to do it because it was something that I always wanted to do and I was reminded that tomorrow is not a guarantee. "Time waits for no one," as my mother would say.

My husband gave me a laptop for my fortieth birthday and the book that you are holding has come to pass. I can say that writing it has been a wonderful journey of discovery. I had no earthly idea how one becomes an author. I'm finding out that in many cases, writing is not a career path that is pursued, but one that is uncovered. It's like opening Grandma's cedar chest and finding treasures that, even though you are looking at them for the first time, are strangely familiar. They are a part of your history. They are part of your DNA, and they are a part of what makes you "YOU." So, I took what I had and I did what I could!

I wrote this book so I could get the giggles out of my head and into your hands. I hope you have laughed with me, at me, and at yourself because laughter makes it all a little easier!! I also hope that along the way, you too were inspired to do the best that you can with whatever you have!

Make a Million Moms
Laugh Anyway Challenge

Okay, moms, I have a dream and I am inviting YOU to dream with me for a worthy cause. I know that when moms come together, THINGS GET DONE! So if you enjoyed this book, laughed-out-loud, were inspired by something I wrote, I am asking you to **spread the love to at least 10 other moms**. Tell your friends, your neighbors, your sisters, your sister's friends and neighbors, your mom, AND your kid's bus driver (she/he will love the story about the Big Yellow Savior) about Laugh Anyway Mom. And, make sure you tell your Facebook friends, Twitter followers, and other social media gal pals about what we are doing.

Every time a copy of Laugh Anyway Mom is purchased, a generous donation from the proceeds of each book goes to help moms and their families through Habitat for Humanity – Will County. This organization provides hope through housing and Laugh Anyway Mom provides hope through humor.

My goal is to make over a million moms laugh every year with my message. And, by doing that through selling books, I'm able to raise funds for those moms who need affordable housing. Imagine the smile on a mom's face and the peace in her heart as she tucks her kids in on their first night in their very own home.

Join me! Together, let's **"Make a Million Moms Laugh Anyway."** It takes just two minutes to spread the love and encourage other moms to join our effort as we help moms reclaim the joy in motherhood!

Make Sure Your Laughter Counts!

1. Go to my website **www.TracyDeGraaf.com** and click on the Make a Million Laugh Moms Laugh Anyway Challenge button.
2. Once you have filled out the simple form, we will verify your purchase and make a contribution to Habitat for Humanity – Will County. Be sure to complete the form so that your purchase will count toward our Million Moms goal.
3. In addition, you'll receive a bonus gift when you post a tweet using #millionmoms at the end of your message. We have made an easy one click link that you can click on to auto post the tweet once you have submitted the Make a Million Moms Laugh Anyway challenge form.

Thank you for helping me spread the love. God bless you and your family.

With Kindness,

Tracy

THE BOYS and me! This photo was taken on Mother's Day 2008 at Six Flags Great America in Gurnee, IL. We had the BEST MOTHER'S DAY EVER!!!

Clockwise from top left: Nate, Luke, Adam, Caleb, Joel and me.

WE CARE SURVEY!

If you have enjoyed this book, please help us serve you better and meet your changing needs by taking a few minutes to complete this survey. You can complete this page and mail it to us at P.O. Box 154, Frankfort, IL, 60423. (We LOVE getting good old fashioned MAIL!) Or, go to our website at www.TracyDeGraaf.com to complete it online. As a special "Thank You" we'll send you exciting news about interesting books and products and a valuable Gift Certificate. *It's Our Pleasure to Serve You!*

Full Name: _____

Complete Address: _____

_____

Best Phone Number to Reach You: _____

Email: _____

(1) Gender (please place X on line in front of your answers): _____ Female _____ Male

(2) Age:____18-25____26-35____36-45____46-55 ____56-65____65+

(3) Marital status: ____Married ____Divorced ____ Single ____Widowed

(4) Is this book: ____Purchased for self? ____Purchased for others? ____Received as gift? (If gift, what was the occasion? _____

(5) How did you find out about this book?____Catalog ____Store Display ____Blog Site ____ Facebook ____ Twitter ____ Other Social Media ____Article ____TV/Talk Show ____Radio/Talk Show ____Word of Mouth ____Professional Referral ____Other (Please Specify)_____

(6) What subjects do you enjoy reading most? (Rank from 1-8 in order of enjoyment.) ____Relationship with opposite sex ____Relationship with children ____Diet/Nutrition/Exercise/Health ____Biz Self

Help _____ Balance Work and Family _____ Getting
Organized _____ Money _____ Spiritual

*Additional Comments you would like to make to help us
serve you better.*

_____

_____

_____

_____

_____

_____

_____

_____

_____

_____

Now moms can have the support they need to lose weight once and for all!

Jennifer Rundall BEFORE and
AFTER losing 75 pounds!

Dear Readers,

I hope you enjoyed reading *LAUGH ANYWAY MOM*. I hope it made you laugh, made you cry, and inspired you to find deeper joy in your life!

I want to introduce you to my new friend Jennifer Rundall. I have struggled with the ups and downs of weight for pretty much my entire adult life (especially after having FIVE healthy baby boys). I'm convinced that my fat has a GPS with my hips programmed into the "go home" button. I've lost the same 25 pounds eight thousand times! UGH!

So, I decided to hire Jennifer as my weight loss coach and she has been fantastic! She has lost over 75 pounds and has kept it off, and now is teaching me to do the same! Jennifer has helped me to take a look at my life as a whole in order to identify areas that I need to change. Small changes can make a big impact in the area of weight. Big changes can put your butt into a whole new orbit—a much smaller one!

Jennifer uses a healthy approach that is gradual and consistent. No fad diets. No pills. No starving yourself. In fact, she doesn't even use the "D" word. She points out that "diet" has the word "die" in it, and she is about living and enjoying life. She really is great and if you have struggled with weight, I highly recommend Jennifer!

You can contact Jennifer by calling 1+602-670-9383 and be sure to check out her website at www.thinspirationcoaching.com and read her story and see my before and after photos too! ;o)

With Kindness,
Tracy DeGraaf

Recommended Resources

The following have played an important role in making this book possible. They are people for whom I hold the highest regard and respect. I recommend them to anyone in need of their products or services.

I recommend any books by the amazing and inspirational Ms. Phyllis Diller. And I LOVE the YouTube.com series interviews that Mr. Fred Westbrook did with Ms. Diller. You cannot watch this and NOT be inspired! She came from a small Midwestern town and started her career in comedy when she was middle aged and had five children. Sound familiar? I just love her!!! Find her books on Amazon.com and the interviews on YouTube.com

Tracey Trottenberg, Leadership Coach and Consultant www.traceytrottenberg.com

Maria Simone, Conscious Business Development Expert www.passion2prosperity.com

Steve and Bill Harrison's Quantum Leap Program, Million Dollar Author Club, National Publicity Summit, Radio-TV Interview Report www.rtir.com

Janet and Landy DeField, Internet Marketing Consultants, Social Networking Coaches and Website Designers www.synergyinternetmarketing.com

Jack Canfield, America's #1 Success Coach www.jackcanfield.com

Brian Tracy, Bestselling Author and International Speaker and President of Brian Tracy University, a private on-line University for sales and entrepreneurship
www.briantracy.com

Jennifer Rundall, Weight Loss Coach and Virtual Assistant Administrative Services www.thinspirationcoaching.com and www.myvadiva.com

E.D. Hill, National TV News Journalist www.hillfriends.com

Pam Boas, The Tony Stewart Foundation www.tonystewartfoundation.org

Lenann McGookey Gardner, Management Consultant www.youcansell.com

Amy Pedersen, Speaker, Author and Co-creator of Slimpressions shapewear www.amypedersen.com and www.themiracleofme.com and www.slimpressions.com

George Foster, Book Cover Designer www.fostercovers.com

Kimberly Carter, Illustrator www.paperheartpress.com

Teri Hawkins, Speaker and Entrepreneur Coach www.NationalEntreprenuersClub.com

Michael Issac, Comedian/Comedy Coach www.michaelissac. com

Dr. Scott Stratton, Chiropractor, Wellness Physician, and Muscle Response Expert www.drscottstratton.com

Elizabeth Ridley, Author, Ghost Writer, Publishing Consultant www.writersmidwife.com

Laura Vander Ploeg, Coach, Author & Keynote www. birdseyeview.us

Karen Ehman, Professional Organizer www.karenehman.com

Debbye Cannon, Professional Organizer http:// BizMomMentor.com

Jeni Ozark, Professional Organizer and Interior Re-Design www.sassyspacesinc.com

Rebecca Palumbo, Principal Creative Director of Rollins Palumbo Creative www.rollinspalumbo.com

David W. Ping, Executive Director Equipping Ministries International www.equippingministries.org

Paula Fellingham, CEO of the Women's Information Network www.thewinonline.com

By the way, be sure to check out my web show on The Women's Information Network at http://thewinonline. com/shows/ugh-raising-boys-show. You will love it!

Who Is Tracy DeGraaf?

Tracy DeGraaf is an author, speaker, web show host, humorist, stand-up comedienne, entrepreneur, and mother of FIVE who inspires people to LAUGH ANYWAY and make the best of every situation, no matter what! Her dynamic and entertaining presentations bring a positive and inspirational message to each audience. She encourages people everywhere to embrace life's rewards and life's challenges with a hope-filled perspective. And, she does it all with a sense of humor!

Tracy has a degree in journalism and public relations from Illinois State University. She has been trained at the Second City in Chicago, and has been called "The Queen of Mom-Comedy" when performing stand-up. She is a small business owner and has years of experience as a top manager in the direct selling industry. The DeGraaf family live in the Chicago area.

Tracy is available as an emcee and she conducts keynote presentations, workshops, breakout sessions, and stand-up comedy for events at colleges, churches, nonprofit organizations, direct sales companies, and corporations.

To contact Tracy for further information about her books, additional products, and The Laugh Anyway Mom's Club, or to schedule her for a presentation, visit www.tracydegraaf.com or www.laughanywaymom.com.